BUT WHY, ROSWITA

ISBN: 978-0-9825086-7-1

First Edition

Published by Fiction Publishing, Inc.
5626 Travelers Way
Fort Pierce, FL 34982

BUT WHY, ROSWITA

A NOVEL BY

PETER HAASE

PART I
May Bacchus never let you sleep alone.

PART II
A slender girl with tousled white-blond hair

PART III
It will be great to be rich.

PART IV
But why, Roswita?

PART I

May Bacchus never let you sleep alone

Chapter One

He set down his suitcase. After a night in a third class compartment on the train, his sleepless, reddened eyes squinted across the wide plaza in front of him. The enormous Hauptbahnhof he had just exited spewed throngs of hurrying pedestrians with luggage and briefcases out into the blinding sunlight, while others hastened toward the gray terminal building, to be swallowed by the dimness of its interior.

The early hour on this August morning already promised scorching heat to descend over the city. The screeching of streetcars battled with engine noises of trucks and blaring automobile horns. Blue exhaust fumes hung in the air. Baggage handlers yelled cautions as they maneuvered their pushcarts through the crowd of arriving and departing travelers. "Coming through! Watch your back! Hey there, move over!"

Uncertain, standing in midst the rushing multitude, the young man looked back at the huge portals of the railroad station as if they were the last link to the world he knew. He had cut the umbilical cord to the familiarity of the small town he had left the evening before. Floating in a hostile sea of humanity, deprived of a life vest, his survival seemed to him in peril.

Again he faced the bustling Bahnhofsplatz with the menacing facades of buildings on the far side: multistoried hotels, banks, department stores and commercial companies. Oversized flags hung lifeless from their poles in the still air; huge letters over canopied entrances announced the purposes of their existence; imposing doorways dwarfed the liveried doormen under their arches.

Small kiosks stood huddled together on one side of the square. One offered newspapers and magazines for the early travelers; another sold cigarettes and bottled beverages, yet another advertised currency exchange in several languages. On one of the kiosks, a sign with large letters read: Rooms for Rent.

Hungry, but without appetite, thirsty and with dry mouth and throat, headache extending from the nape of his neck over his skull and into the eyes, he picked up his suitcase and started in the direction of the kiosks. He did not know how long he would have to live on the sixty-five marks in his pocket, so he passed by the kiosk selling drinks. Pausing at the newspaper stand, he decided against buying a paper and headed for the one that promised rooms for rent. It had the appearance of a somewhat more permanent establishment, an office, with a door.

Before entering, he studied the notices pasted on the door and the single window. A colorful sign read: Rooms! Rooms! Rooms! There were addresses, meaningless to him; some posters had pictures. Large red letters proclaimed: Rent by the Day, Week or Month! Low Prices! Low Deposits!

All this was so new to him, so strange, so alien. Where or when did he ever have to find a place to rest, to sleep, to set down his suitcase? To lie down and ease his headache? Where or when had he been uncertain about his next meal or a drink? Where or when had there ever been a doubt that everything was taken care of?

Reluctantly, intimidated by the overpowering pulse of the big city, his hand reached for the doorknob. Courage, I have to do something, he told himself. Through the glass he saw a man and a woman behind a counter. He pushed at the door, but it did not yield. Quickly he realized he had to pull. First mistake. He blushed over his clumsiness. With a firm grip on his suitcase, he entered and stood in the narrow space between the entrance and the counter.

"Need a room? A place to stay? For a day or a week?" The man's voice did not sound unfriendly, but also not too sympathetic. He would certainly not be interested in the story of somebody who just arrived on a train, had a headache, was tired, hungry and thirsty.

"I just arrived by train and I am starting a job, an apprentice job really, in the fur trade in Niddastrasse. That's near here, right? I need a place, a room, something…"

"For a month, then? We don't have long-term accommodations. Want a room for a month?"

"If it's not too expensive. I have only …"

"The fee is seven marks," and to the woman, "give him a list." With that he shoved a form and a pencil across the counter top. "Put your name here and sign it. It says you received five addresses. That's it. You got the seven marks?"

The young man counted out the money, printed Walter Hansen on the form and signed it. He left the Rooms-for-Rent agency with a receipt and a typewritten list of addresses.

Desperate for a place to sit, Walter found a bench at the bus stop in front of one of the hotels. With the suitcase between his feet, he sat and became aware again of the throbbing pain in his head. He unfolded the map of Frankfurt, which he had bought at the gift shop inside the station, to find the street names on the list the agent had given him. Then, ignoring the headache and overcoming his lethargy, he made the effort to rise from the bench and once again pick up his suitcase. With map and address list in his free hand, he began to walk across the wide plaza.

He found the address on the top of his list and rang the doorbell. A window opened on the first floor. "Yes? What is it?" An elderly woman looked down on him.

"The room? I want to rent the room you have."

"It's rented." She withdrew from the window.

"But it says here…" he protested against the closing window.

Next on his list, a few houses down the street, there was no answer. At the third address he actually had a conversation with a middle-aged woman, who complained about the agency. "They keep sending me people. I told them, don't send me more people, it's rented. Go, tell them it's rented."

"Sorry," he said. Back on the street, his courage dwindled and his suitcase grew heavier.

"Our renter is moving out tomorrow," Frau Landsberg at the next address told him. "You can sleep on the couch in the living room for one night, if you want to."

4

"Thank you. I have another address."

But there was no room there either. There had never been one.

Around the corner, a large showroom window had in gold lettering *Mittagstisch* on it, and underneath: Lunch served from twelve to three. Weekly rates. Reasonable. Walter entered.

"Today we have mock-turtle soup. Roulades, potatoes and spinach. Ice cream." The waiter was in a hurry; it was almost three o'clock and there was no one else in the lunchroom. "You can pay by the meal or by the week," he said.

"I don't know yet…"

"Just for today, then." He put a glass of water on the table, and Walter drank eagerly. He wished he had a couple of aspirins.

With surprising speed the waiter brought the soup, which was tasty. Walter ate slowly and, the bowl still half full, a plate of roulades, mashed potato and leafy spinach was set before him.

"Beer?" the waiter asked.

"No, thank you. Ah, you wouldn't have an aspirin, would you?"

"This is not a pharmacy, my friend." He laughed at his own cleverness. "The pharmacy is across the street. You want your ice cream now?"

Walter nodded and the waiter came back with two scoops of vanilla ice cream. "That'll be three fifty."

The fume-laden air vibrated in the afternoon heat as he walked back to the address where there was at least a couch, where he could put his aching head on a pillow, where he could leave his suitcase. Landsberg was her name, he remembered. She seemed friendly, I'll be able to rest; any place will do.

"Ah, you came back, huh? Well, it's too early. You see, I have people here, a party. You can come in the evening, nine or ten. Okay?" She saw Walter's pale face. "Are you all right?"

"Yes. It's just... I haven't slept... and..."

"I am sorry. Maybe eight o'clock, okay? You can leave your suitcase. We'll put it here in the corner."

His arms and shoulders felt feather-light as he left the house. Consulting his map again, he directed his steps to Niddastrasse, a block or two away. He had come to Frankfurt to begin his apprenticeship in the fur trade.

The street was one big construction site. Raw, gray buildings of five or six stories, unfinished, entire facades missing, were in the early stages of completion. The pavement was broken up, sewage pipes and materials lay around in disorderly heaps. Cement trucks, heavy machinery and bulldozers moved noisily between piles of dug-up dirt, coils of cables and steaming asphalt containers, giving off the sharp smell of tar.

Among the workers in overalls and hard hats, there were others, wearing white smocks, incongruous in this surrounding, stepping gingerly over puddles and around materials and equipment. They stood in groups, talking, many of them carrying bundles of furs; they entered and left the unfinished buildings. They were the fur merchants in this center of the European fur trade.

Carefully, not to get his shoes muddy—he wanted to make a good impression when he met his new boss—Walter advanced toward a group of men in white smocks, the traditional attire of the fur merchants.

"Excuse me, where can I find Herr Pinkert? Hans Pinkert?"

"Pinkert?" one of them asked. "I don't know where he is." He looked from one to the other of his companions.

"Pinkert?" someone said. "Isn't he with Leo Reichenberg? Yeah, he is in the next building, second or third floor. Ask somebody there. They'll know."

"Thanks." Walter made his way around a cement mixer, sidestepped a muddy puddle and walked through the wide opening into the building. On the second floor he met a young man in a white smock with a bundle of Persian lamb skins over his shoulder.

"Hans Pinkert in this building?" asked Walter.

"Yeah, upstairs."

And there it was: Leo Reichenberg, hand printed, and underneath, Hans Pinkert. He found what he came for. Confidently he pulled the heavy door open. The loft-like room, here called a lager, was enormous, with a long window front. Stacks of furs sat on the floor and on tables. Bundles hung from the ceiling.

Martin Geier turned around. He pushed the light green visor he wore on his forehead to the top of his head to better see who had come in. His white smock was stained a bluish black down the front. The wide table under the window front, at which he was working, was piled from end to end with stacks

7

of black furs. As he came closer, Walter saw that they were Persian lamb.

"Is this where I will find Herr Pinkert? Herr Hans Pinkert?" He knew Pinkert was in his fifties, but the person in front of him was not much older than he himself, perhaps in his mid-twenties.

"You must be the new one Herr Pinkert expects. Hi, I am Martin Geier."

"Walter Hansen. Pleased to meet you." They shook hands.

Geier returned to his work. Over his shoulder he explained, "I have to finish this. They're sold to Vienna. Sorted and bundled. Know anything about sorting?"

"No. Well, a little. I have watched my father."

"You distinguish patterns, structure—character, we call it. No two skins of the same character, like fingerprints. They're unique. Look, I show you. See this? Compare. Different, right? More like this one. The curl tighter, firmer, longer. So, you put it on this pile. Next. Oh, those I have at the end over there. You have your smock with you? Where are you staying? Pinkert's not here right now; you'll see him later. I work for Leo Reichenberg."

Walter was not in any condition to absorb what talkative Martin Geier rattled on and on about. "I have not been able to unpack yet. I found a place, but…"

"Good. Near here, I hope. Can you bring that stack over here? I have to start on those now. See, you're already helping. Pinkert will like that. How much is the rent? You had to put down a deposit?"

"I don't know yet. Couldn't talk to the lady. She had people there. I'll find out in the evening."

Geier shrugged his shoulders and went on sorting the Persian lambs.

"It may be temporary until I find a more permanent place," Walter added. He stood aside and watched, helped move a stack of skins from the floor to the table and slowly began to grasp the concept of bringing together skins of similar character. Eventually they would be sold to furriers in packages, or bundles, of twenty-four or twenty-six skins.

Wearing a clean white smock, Hans Pinkert, tall and athletic, although perhaps a little too heavy and too old for an athlete, rushed into the lager. "Oh, good, you are here. You are Herr Hansen, right? Walter Hansen?" With an outstretched arm, he came vigorously toward them, slapping Geier on the shoulder and taking Walter's hand. "I expected you on the first; you're two weeks late. How was that sail? All around Denmark, huh?"

"Yeah, I am sorry, but I couldn't say no to such an offer. It was a one-time opportunity and ..."

Pinkert laughed. "I thought, this fellow has guts. Gets a job and then says: no, first I sail around Denmark." He laughed again. "I liked that. Bold and refreshing."

Walter's hand hurt from the tight grip Hans Pinkert had inflicted on him. He apologized again and said, "It was a great trip. Thanks for understanding."

"So, I see our friend Martin has already taken advantage of you. Where's your smock? Get your clothes dirty from the dye. Come with me to the office." He took Walter by the elbow and they entered the cubicle, provisionally separated from the lager by wood paneling. "This is Frau Kunze. She does all the correspondence, the billing and answers the phone. I am not here much. Always running around."

Walter shook hands with the matronly round Frau Kunze, whose eyes carried a maternal, conspiratorial smile. "Actually I work for Leo Reichenberg, but I help out with the billing and the correspondence. Herr Pinkert doesn't have much work."

Hans Pinkert laughed out loud again. "That will change, now that we have Herr Hansen. May I call you Walter?"

Indeed, Hans Pinkert did not have much work. He also had no merchandise. His business was that of a commissionaire, a common occupation in the fur trade. A commissionaire has clients who rely on his expertise to provide them with the best merchandise at the best prices available on the market.

There are more than a hundred fur wholesalers in Frankfurt, and most of them are located in Niddastrasse, and the commissionaire must know them all. The relationship between the wholesaler and the commissionaire is one of mutual benefit: one has the merchandise, the other the customers.

Pinkert, like an engine energized by a fully charged battery, stormed back into the lager. "Follow me, Walter. Let's get out of here. I'll show you around."

Martin Geier did not look up from his work; he was used to Hans Pinkert's impetuous temperament, but Walter could hardly follow. Weary from the sleepless night and all the new impressions, his headache not quite gone, he longed for a quiet moment to collect his thoughts. Not before eight tonight, he reflected, and it was only mid-afternoon.

"All these buildings were damaged in the war. This one was completely destroyed," said Pinkert as they walked down the stairs. "Careful. No handrails yet. The elevator will be installed next week. That's what they say; I believe it when I see it."

That afternoon Walter met more people than he had known all his life. In the street, on every floor of the buildings they visited, in lofts and offices, even in the coffeehouse they entered for a brief moment to have a cup of coffee, Hans Pinkert introduced him to everyone in a white smock.

Evening came and the activities in Niddastrasse simmered down. Herr Pinkert and Walter returned to the lager. "We have to make a few packages and send them off to customers. You know how to pack? Geier can help you. Frau Kunze types the address labels and the packing slips."

Walter Hansen saw himself standing in line at the railway express office with three parcels, furs Herr Pinkert had collected during the day for his customers. Walter did not yet quite understand how this business worked and, he told himself, I can't learn it all in one day, especially this first afternoon after a sleepless night, and he looked forward to starting out fresh in the morning.

Back at the coffeehouse he had visited earlier with Herr Pinkert, Walter ordered a slice of meat pie and a soda. There were still a few men in white smocks, coming and going, some nodding or waving in his direction, some even said, "Hey, Walter," and he answered as if he had an idea who they were. He realized how tired he was, but it was only six thirty and he did not want to ring the bell at exactly eight o'clock.

Careful as he was, it had been impossible to keep his shoes clean. Mud had dried all around the soles and some of it even on the upper leather. Inside the Hauptbahnhof, in the huge hall of the main railroad station, he remembered, between the flower shop and the gift shop, there was a shoeshine stand. Seventy-five Pfennigs read a sign. Walter sat on the high chair and the old man worked on his shoes, mumbling something about the state of the footwear confronting him. The job finished, Walter handed him a one-mark coin; he did not want the change, nor was it offered.

A few minutes after eight o'clock, he slowly walked across the plaza to Frau Landsberg's apartment, his home for tonight.

Chapter Two

The night on the couch in Frau Landsberg's apartment had not given Walter Hansen the rest he needed so desperately. The air in the living room was heavy with stale cigarette smoke; full ashtrays, empty beer glasses and bottles stood on the tables and on the sideboard.

Frau Landsberg had let him in and then disappeared without saying anything about paying rent and no more than, "Come in. The living room's all yours." From his suitcase in a corner of the corridor he retrieved his toothbrush, found the bathroom and then retreated to the living room. He did not dare to undress, only removed his shoes, took off his jacket and loosened his tie. The couch was uncomfortable; there was a blanket and a cushion, but no sheet. Walter could not extend his legs full length. During the night he tried to accommodate himself by hanging his feet over the side, putting them up on the armrest or bending his knees.

In the morning, before he heard anyone stirring, he visited the bathroom, changed his clothes and then left the apartment. With his white smock over his arm, he headed for the coffee shop at the corner of Niddastrasse. The construction noises began at the stroke of seven and even at this early hour, there were already some people in white smocks. Mostly younger men, they all seemed to know each other, stood in groups, laughing, slapping each other on the shoulders, in a congenial atmosphere.

A plate of French toast and two cups of coffee set him back two fifty, which left him with just fifty marks and some change. Neither his salary nor the rent had been discussed and Walter felt uncertain about his first month away from home.

"Hi. I'm Horst Klein. They call me Pudding around here. You the new guy for Hans Pinkert, right?" One tall, lanky fellow approached Walter and pulled a chair over to join him. "I saw you yesterday with him coming into our lager."

"Right. Walter Hansen." He stretched out his hand. "I remember you." Of course, he didn't; he had seen too many new faces the day before, but was glad that someone came toward him in a friendly manner and he wanted to be equally gracious.

"I work with Arthur Selter, on the floor below you. Stop by at lunchtime. You'll meet some of the other guys." Pudding hurried away and, over his shoulder, called out, "See you then."

Finished with his breakfast, Walter headed for Hans Pinkert's loft, although it seemed to him still too early, climbed the stairs and found Martin Geier already at work, sorting the Persian lambs.

"Pinkert is in the office," Geier said. "He's waiting for you. We start early around here."

Walter quickly shed his jacket and donned the white smock he had brought. The morning went by fast. Together with Herr Pinkert, he visited lager after lager, fur loft after fur loft, inspected all the different merchandise, sorted through newly arrived lots of fox, marten, raccoon, skunk and a variety of lamb and kid skins. All this was done while joking with the owners and personnel, and kidding with the secretaries. What a different world, thought Walter. How will I fit in? They are all friends, it seems to me. How can they conduct serious business in this light-hearted way?

Walter realized they all spoke with a Saxon dialect. He had noticed it when Pudding approached him in the coffee shop. The center of the European fur trade had been Leipzig in Saxony, before that part of Germany was separated from the West by the Iron Curtain. Gradually transferred to Frankfurt, and starting out with the miserable remnants of merchandise smuggled across the border, it was a difficult beginning for most companies. What came with them was of course their heavy, accented dialect—and the unique Saxon humor.

At the lager of Arthur Selter, Walter Hansen met with Pudding, who introduced him to Jürgen Springsguth, a jovial fellow, balding in spite of his young age, and to slightly overweight Rolf Herbert. A moment later, a young woman, petite and brunette, came out of the office.

"Ilse, meet Walter." Pudding put an arm around her. "He's with Pinkert. You'll get to know him better soon enough."

Walter took her hand, "Nice meeting you," while the other two snickered and had their own private joke.

"She knows everyone—I mean everyone," said Jürgen. "Real well. Know what I mean?" They all laughed in common understanding, including Ilse. Rolf Herbert urged them on. "Let's go. I am hungry."

Wehage's Round Table, a cheap diner located a block away at the corner of Mainzer Landstrasse, was frequented by the young crowd of apprentices, traders and commissionaires, heart and soul of the fur business. Open only for lunch, this restaurant, resembling a factory cafeteria, was a rowdy place during the hours from noon to three. With no need for a menu, Wehage's customers ate what he and his wife prepared: one day it was pea soup, pot roast and vanilla pudding, the next potato soup, beef stew and chocolate pudding. There was never a choice. The two sturdy waitresses placed pitchers of artificially flavored lemonade on every table without asking. They served whoever came in and sat at a table, what the kitchen had produced, without asking, and there were no questions, no arguments and no special orders.

Payment was with coupons. Regular diners bought a booklet with ten or twenty-five coupons from which the waitress removed one as soon as she served the soup. If the booklet was not on the table, there would be trouble. Newcomers, like Walter, could pay in cash, but the three marks had better be in clear view when the waitress came around with the soup.

Ilse warned Walter of this procedure. "If you don't have a coupon, put three marks to your right on the table, otherwise you get yelled at. And no tipping."

They found a round table in the center of the large, noisy room and pulled a fifth chair over. Today it was potato soup and beef stew. The chocolate pudding came before they had the time to finish the soup.

Squeezed in at a table normally for four, Walter and his new friends had to talk loudly to make themselves heard over the din of the rambunctious crowd. "Pinkert was waiting for you. Said you first wanted to sail around Denmark. What a nerve! Could have lost that job." Ilse spoke in her strong Saxon dialect that sounded almost humorous to Walter. "What was that like? I've never even been close to the ocean."

"Yeah, I've been sailing since I was a kid." I have to embellish a little on my story, thought Walter. These people seem to want to get a laugh out of everything. "Ten days. We were drunk most of the time." Well, that was pretty much true. "We had some rough weather, but in port we had a lot of fun. Copenhagen, what a town! The Tivoli. Girls all over the place. In Malmø, Sweden, we got into a fight at some dancehall. Then they confiscated our passports because we didn't have visas. They gave us our passports back the next day and we had to leave. We were six guys on the boat. Yeah, was a great trip."

"A fight in Sweden? In a dancehall? How did that happen?" Ilse wanted to know. They all made sure they didn't miss a word of the story.

Walter was beginning to enjoy himself. "That was funny," he continued, "but it almost became serious. One of our guys danced with a girl, and then her boyfriend rushed out onto the dance floor and threw a punch. We were ready to jump in, but then it didn't come to that. Friends of his came out, dragged him back." Walter went on, exaggerating, "the police came, wanted to see IDs. We didn't have a visa in our passports. So, they took us in and kept our passes. Next morning we had to show up and they gave us an hour to leave Sweden."

By the time they finished their meal and had to get back to work, Walter had become one of this group of friends. The afternoon went by fast. Herr Pinkert sent him out, for the first time alone, to find some natural Indian lambs that matched the sample a customer had sent in. His boss told him of a couple of firms where he might have the best chance of finding them. Pinkert approved of what he had brought in and that evening, Walter, happy over his first success, delivered the package to the post office and then went "home" to Frau Landsberg's apartment.

Frau Landsberg met him at the door. "Ach, Herr Hansen, there has been a misunderstanding. My tenant is not moving out yet. So, I don't have the room for you. I know, it is late. You can sleep another night on the couch. I charge you only two marks per night. Is that all right with you? Sorry. Or do you have another place?"

The good feeling he had about his job and the friends he made over lunch evaporated. He was tired, had not yet completely overcome the impact of all the new impressions of his first two days in this big city. All day long, the anticipation of having his own room—a room he had not even seen—had kept his spirit up.

"Another place? No, I don't have another place." He asked if he could have a key and she gave him one. Dejected and lonely, he went out to find something to eat, and at a street corner he bought a frankfurter from a vendor.

Walter felt a slap on his shoulder. He turned and found himself face to face with Rolf Herbert.

"What you standing around here eating on the street," Rolf grinned. "Come, tonight we meet at Anagnostopolis for a bottle of wine or two. The other guys will be there. Ilse too. She likes you. But she likes anybody with balls," he laughed.

Together they walked the couple of blocks to Hochstrasse and, a few steps down, entered a cellar *Lokal*. Over the door hung a brass vine of grapes, reflecting the low rays of the setting sun, and the curlicue lettering *Anagnostopolis*. The room was dark and smoky; the eyes had to adjust before they could discern tables, chairs and people. It was not crowded, as the evening was still young. A waitress in a short white skirt and shorter wine-colored apron greeted them. They selected a table under a lamp hanging from the low vaulted ceiling, emitting a purplish glow.

Their friends had not yet arrived. Taking their seats, Rolf repeated the question he had asked on their way over to Anagnostopolis. "So, what's the problem? You look kind of *verorschelt?*"

That must be Saxon for *verorgelt*, Walter translated in his mind, meaning something like you've been through the wringer. "Yeah, there's a problem. I don't have a place to sleep. Slept one night on a couch, now that woman tells me, I could sleep another night on the couch. Then it's... I don't know."

"Oh that. Yeah, I know what you're talking about. We all went through that when we first came over here from the East. Jürgen and I slept the first couple of weeks in a bombed-out house, in a tent."

Jürgen Springsguth came in and joined them. "What? No place to sleep? They threw you out already? Tried to screw the landlady, huh? And her husband didn't like it, huh?" He laughed. "At least they let you stay another night."

Rolf laughed, too. Then he said reassuringly, "We'll come up with something."

The waitress asked for their order. "Want the wine list?"

Jürgen spoke for them. "We're still waiting for more people. In the meantime, bring us a plate of *Handkäs mit Musik*." He liked this Frankfurter specialty, rolls of ripe Harzer cheese with a dressing of vinegar and chopped onion.

He nodded toward Walter. "Hey, Ilse has a double bed. She'd be glad for the company." Again they laughed and Walter joined in, half-heartedly.

"Double bed? Company? What are you talking about?" Ilse had arrived with Pudding. "I have no shortage of company."

"Our friend Walter is in a kind of dilemma. They threw him out," Rolf informed them. "Tried funny business with the landlady," followed by another salvo of laughter.

A dilemma all right, but Walter couldn't help being swept along with the hilarity of this unruly band of people who took nothing seriously, found a joke in everything.

When they were all seated, they ordered a bottle of *Insel Samos*, a sweet Greek dessert wine—the cheapest on the wine list. It was not the first time that they had come to Anagnostopolis and often they had to count out their last pfennigs to settle the bill. Munching on the Handkäs and tiny slices of dark bread, they filled the glasses and welcomed Walter properly into their group, proposing toasts of a more or less raunchy nature.

"May Bacchus never let you sleep alone," offered Jürgen. Rolf Herbert raised his glass. "May the women who drink with you show their appreciation—know what I mean?" Pudding followed with, "Most of all, may you never fall into the hands of the husband whose wife you are sleeping with," and Ilse finished in her funny Saxon dialect, "May all the girls be as good looking in the morning as the evening before."

"Thanks," answered Walter, "I drink to all your good wishes. But, seriously, I don't know what I will do after tonight. I may have to sleep in the lager on a bunch of Persian lamb, or skunk or something."

20

"I may have a solution." Jürgen thought for a moment. "I painted the apartment for a woman in Adalbertstrasse, when I first came here from Leipzig. For extra cash. Frau Kohl is her name. Never had the time to finish the job, so she won't talk to me. She has a room she wants to rent out. You look trustworthy. Maybe we can persuade her. Want to go tomorrow at lunch time?"

"Yeah, sure. Frau Kohl? Adal-what Strasse? Where's that?"

"It's a twenty-minute walk, Adalbertstrasse 45. It's a long shot. She's a feisty woman, but has a good heart. Want to try? I think she said seventy-five a month."

"Sounds good, but I don't have seventy-five marks. You think Pinkert might give me an advance?"

"Pinkert's okay that way. He'll help you out."

After a second bottle of Insel Samos, Walter said good night to his friends. Walking unsteadily after all that wine and only a frankfurter and a few bites of Handkäs in his stomach, he felt for the key in his pocket to reassure himself that he had a place to sleep for at least one more night.

Frau Landsberg met him at the door as he entered. "Where have you been? It's almost midnight. I waited up for you. You owe me four marks, you know. I sleep late in the mornings, so you better pay me now."

"You don't have to be so hostile. I pay you. First you tell me you have a room, but then you don't. And now *you* don't trust *me*?" Walter, emboldened by the wine, had found the courage to raise his voice. Besides, he now had friends and Hans Pinkert would certainly advance him some money. Tomorrow he would move into a room at... what's the name of that street? Frau what's-her-name? He counted out four marks and handed the money over to the woman. "Now leave me alone. I need to sleep. I have a job, you know. Not like some people who don't have to get up in the morning."

Stretched out, as far as the couch permitted, Walter thought of Ilse. Pretty, he thought. That laugh, so uninhibited. She likes me, Rolf said. But she likes anyone with... She seems to be with Pudding. Someone like that...

He fell asleep.

Chapter Three

Frau Kohl, in her mid-to late fifties and a good thirty pounds overweight, was a feisty one, all right. When Jürgen Springsguth and Walter Hansen rang her doorbell the following day at noontime, she received them with a torrent of offensive language.

"You dare show your face? It took me a week to clean up after you. Nothing is finished. Look at the wall behind the fridge. And the trim above the counter. You never even started on the bathroom. And I paid you."

"I'm sorry, Frau Kohl, but actually you owe..."

"What? I owe you nothing. You have the nerve..."

"No, no, Frau Kohl, it's all right. You owe me nothing, if only you let me explain. You see..." Jürgen had no explanation that would satisfy the woman.

Walter jumped in. "Frau Kohl, I am Walter Hansen. Herr Springsguth told me the whole story. That's why I am..."

"Herr Springsguth? Herr Springsguth? Nix Herr Springsguth. He left me hanging in this mess, and now..."

"That's why I am here, Frau Kohl. Herr Springsg..., eh, Jürgen, he became ill and so he couldn't... The paint and all... The thing is, Frau Kohl, if I finish for you where he left off... Frau Kohl, I need a room. I rent the room you have, and then I finish..."

"What? You're a friend of his? Why should I trust you?"

"Frau Kohl," Jürgen interjected, "Herr Hansen just came to Frankfurt. He has a good job. He's a good worker, reliable and trustworthy. You'll see. And, if he promises you to finish with the painting and I'll help..."

"You help? I don't want anything more to do with you." She nodded toward Walter. "He seems okay. Do you smoke? No smoking here. What was your name?"

"Walter Hansen, Frau Kohl. Pleased to meet you. And I don't smoke."

"Let's see then. When do you want to move in? It's seventy-five down now and then every first it's seventy-five. Got the money?"

"But, Frau Kohl, it's already the seventeenth, and..."

"You want the room? The rest is your deposit. And another thing, the paint is in the basement. You can start right now."

Hans Pinkert had advanced Walter a hundred marks and when they left Frau Kohl at Adalbertstrasse 45, Walter had barely fifty marks in his pocket. "This is for the two remaining weeks in August," Pinkert had told him. "After that it's two hundred at the end of every month. So, go carefully. You don't get your next pay until the end of September. I guess you brought some money from home to tide you over, right? If not, you better write to your father."

"Write to my father," Walter repeated to Jürgen. "Not much hope there. He thinks he gave me a fortune with that train ticket and some bills he happened to have on him when he sent me off. How can I live on fifty marks for six weeks?

And," he asked without expecting an answer, "next month's rent? Where's that gonna come from?"

They passed Wehage's Round Table on their way back to Niddastrasse. "Too late for lunch now," said Jürgen. It was almost three when they came back to work, but Jürgen went on, "You will find the hours in this business flexible. In the evenings you'll work sometimes to eight or nine o'clock. Post office, railway express, stuff like that."

In the afternoon, Walter had only a couple of errands to run and then take some packages to the post office. Frau Kunze typed the labels and gave him the money for the postage. "So, you have a room now. I'm glad for you," she said with motherly concern. "And you get to go home early today."

"Thanks." Walter picked up the suitcase he had left in Frau Kunze's office and began the long walk to Adalbertstrasse. The last time I lug this thing around.

His room had a narrow but comfortable bed, a little coffee table with an armchair, an old bureau and some hooks on the wall from which to hang his pants and jackets. Hidden in an alcove behind a curtain was a sink with warm and cold water. Frau Kohl told him there was a bathtub in the basement. He went down and found a rusty tub and a garden hose. No hot water. Better than nothing, he told himself.

At last he could unpack his suitcase. On Saturday, Walter began painting Frau Kohl's bathroom. They exchanged a few polite words and Frau Kohl seemed to forget her distrust. Hesitantly at first, she disclosed that she had recently lost her husband, Laszlo, to emphysema. "He smoked four packs a day," she told him. "Everything smelled of cigarettes.

The curtains, the cushions, the rugs, the couch... I want to throw it all out. That's why I want new paint on the walls. You understand?"

"Yes, Frau Kohl, I understand. And, as I told you already, I don't smoke, so..."

"And no visitors after ten, and no ladies over night. Is that clear?"

"Yes, of course, Frau Kohl."

"So we understand each other. Don't get that paint all over the floor. I had a mess here when your friend didn't show up any more."

Most of the young men and women engaged in one or another capacity in the fur trade had found lodgings in the vicinity of Niddastrasse, the center of the European fur market. Pudding—Walter never found out what had earned Horst Klein that unlikely nickname—lived a block away from Hauptbahnhof, behind the railway tracks leading into the terminal. His landlady allowed him to use the kitchen and pretty much the whole apartment, as she was often absent for days at a time, and his place was the most convenient one for the friends to get together.

Pudding, the oldest of the group by a couple of years, worked in the lager of Arthur Selter. He was the highest paid among the friends. Ilse, his girlfriend at the time of Walter's arrival in Frankfurt, was the secretary in Selter's firm. It was not quite clear where she lived, only that she moved often. When the friends came together for an evening of poker or to listen to the latest jazz albums, she was usually there.

"Don't throw away your bottles," Rolf Herbert announced one evening as he arrived at Pudding's place. "I found this great little shop where an old man sells cheap *Wein vom Fass*. You have to bring your own bottle. Here, I bought two." He took one bottle from a paper bag. "Bordeaux or something. I tasted it. Pretty good for two marks." He set the bottle on the table where they had just begun a game of poker.

"Wein vom Fass?" Ilse asked.

"Yeah, he has these big vats, huge casks. Siphons it out with a rubber hose."

"Let me see that." Pudding reached for the bottle. "Is that stuff any good?"

"Pour some of it in this mug," said Jürgen while Pudding smelled the cork.

"You don't have to smell the cork. That's an old cork from another bottle," Rolf laughed.

"Hm, not too bad." Jürgen smacked his lips. "But that aftertaste. Sour, bitter, rotten... Here, Ilse, take a sip. You have great taste buds. What do you think?"

"My taste buds say no." She made a face as sour as the wine. "Vat, siphon—I don't like the sound of it." She handed the mug back to Jürgen who took another mouthful. "Anyway, what do you know about my taste buds, huh?"

"They're great! You have great tasting taste buds. I know, I tasted them!" And to Rolf, "You agree? You know what I'm talking about."

"Great taste buds!" Rolf asserted, vigorously nodding his head.

They all laughed—well, Pudding not quite so much. Ilse gave him a hug. "You like my taste buds, right? You know them better than anyone." She gave him a kiss.

"Yeah. Enough about taste buds. Let's get back to the wine. Hey Jürgen, give me that mug," Pudding demanded. He

27

sniffed. "You drink this stuff?" He took a small sip. "Well, I guess I can get used to it."

Walter came in late. He had finished painting the wall behind Frau Kohl's refrigerator and touching up here and there. "What are you drinking?"

"Wine siphoned from some old man's vat. Have some," Ilse sang out in her melodious Saxon dialect. "Let's test your taste buds." Her frivolous laughter followed.

"Told you," Rolf nudged Walter. "She likes you," he whispered loudly enough for everyone to hear.

"Again with the taste buds," Pudding mumbled. "Will you guys cut it out?"

"Oh come on, Pudding. We're just having fun."

"Yeah, yeah. All right, let's play some poker."

Jürgen asked Walter, "Did Frau Kohl give you any money, now that you finished the job?"

"Twenty marks."

"That's ten bottles of wine!" Rolf calculated everything by how many drinks you could buy. "Or four bottles of Insel Samos at Anagnostopolis."

"Come on, deal the cards," Pudding insisted. "Ilse, go get some glasses from the kitchen. Anything you can find."

"Spit in the Ocean, jokers are wild." Jürgen shuffled and then dealt the cards.

Ilse came back with an assortment of marmalade, mayonnaise and mustard jars. "Here, who needs stemware for wine siphoned from an old man's vat."

Rolf poured the wine and they began playing. Ilse sat between Pudding and Jürgen, looking into both their cards. She did not play, nor did she understand the game, but blurted out, "Oh, two kings!" and then, "Are those sevens any good?

Will three of them beat his kings?" She sipped some of Pudding's wine, made a face and set the glass down. "I have a few coins. Can I bet, too?"

They set the limit at fifty pfennigs. After a few games, Jürgen was the first to run out of money and he wrote a big 50 and his initials on a slip of paper. Pudding, who had won a couple of times, accepted the IOU and advanced Jürgen the money.

They played, drank the wine and Rolf took the second bottle from the bag. Ilse didn't care for the wine and gave up after trying it a few times. "It's awful. I don't know how you guys can drink that stuff."

"Yeah, pretty bad," said Walter and he also stopped drinking, fearing it might give him a headache. Rolf and Jürgen did not seem to care and guzzled down glass after glass, quickly getting drunk.

Soon Pudding and Walter had coins piled up in front of them, while Rolf and Jürgen were broke. More slips of paper were issued. Before they had finished the two bottles of wine, they played almost exclusively with IOUs in various amounts and lost track of who owed what to whom. They did away with the fifty-pfennig limit, played on and wrote paper slips in ever increasing amounts.

Late that evening, Rolf and Jürgen assisted each other as they stumbled along the sidewalks, joking about Isle's taste buds and the wine siphoned from the old man's cask, laughing uproariously. Walter and Ilse walked along with them to their door. She hooked her arm under his as they continued to the apartment house where she lived.

"You want to come up?" asked Ilse.

Walter would have liked nothing more than that. But what about Pudding? My new friends? I just came here. I'm lucky to have friends. No, I can't do that. How can she even ask?

"Ah, well... I think, I'd better go home. Not that I wouldn't like to... But, you know..."

"Those two old ladies I live with are deaf as bats—they don't hear a thing."

"No, Ilse, it's not that. I mean, I'm glad I met you and the others and... and especially Pudding. I don't think it would be right."

"All right then, maybe next time." She flung her arms around him, pressed her body against his and kissed him. Walter thought of her taste buds.

On his long walk home to Adalbertstrasse he reasoned with himself. Should I have...? No, I did the right thing. What would Rolf or Jürgen have done? Oh, they probably have already. I'm sure they think I went with her. Damn... I don't know. I am from a small town. Things must be different in the big city. And anyway, she said maybe next time.

Walter entered quiet as a church mouse, not to disturb Frau Kohl. What am I afraid of? he thought. I am an adult, I can come home as late as I want. In his pocket he found some coins and a bunch of paper slips, various amounts and initials on them. Probably useless; I'm not going to ask them to pay up. Ah, dammit, Ilse... What should I have done? No, no, I did the right thing.

Martin Geier was already at work when Walter arrived at Leo Reichenberg's loft and Frau Kunze was opening the early mail. "There's a ton of work for you. Herr Pinkert might not be coming in today."

"Good morning to you, too, Frau Kunze." He reached for the letters. "Let me see. Rabbit, seal... Gris fox, those I get right here from Reichenberg. For the Indian lamb I try Thorer & Hollender first. Then maybe Westfell. I'll get right to it." Geier helped him select a bundle of gris foxes. For the rabbit and the sealskins, Walter's best chance to find what he needed for his customers was at Interfurs. Both Rolf Herbert and Jürgen Springsguth were apprentices at Interfurs, a large international company with headquarters in London. Not too eager to see Rolf and Jürgen, Walter left that job for the afternoon.

The most difficult task was to find the Indian lambs for a customer in Hannover who was hard to please. Natural gray, he had specified, and first quality. Walter went to see the entire inventory of Indian lamb at Thorer & Hollender and then, for comparison, at Westfell. Not yet an expert—far from it—he sorted through dozens of bundles, set aside some for closer inspection and relied on the advice of the personnel. Still unsure, he went back to Thorer & Hollender and selected two bundles he considered within the customer's specification. Both were of fine quality, one of them slightly less expensive.

"Good job," Frau Kunze praised him as he came back to the office with the merchandise. "Herr Pinkert would like that."

"He is a nice man, I really like him," said Walter.

"He is a nice man, most of the time, but he does have a temper. Unpredictable."

Once Walter overheard a conversation. "He told no one where he was going," someone said, "but I saw him in London. I didn't know what to make of it."

He also learned that his boss had been a prisoner of war in England and that he returned only the year before to Germany. Nineteen forty-nine? He wondered. Four years after the war?

Walter did not want to run into his friends at Wehage's and went to have lunch at the Mittagstisch where he had his first meal on the day he arrived in Frankfurt. That was now two weeks in the past. How desperate and lonely I was then, he thought. Now I have friends and I try to avoid them. How ironic.

Frau Kunze had received some telephone orders, which Walter filled easily, but then he could no longer delay his visit to Interfurs. The very large lager was overflowing with furs of a vast variety, piled on tables, on the floor and hanging from the ceiling. Rolf and Jürgen, engaged in sorting and bundling rabbit skins, looked up as Walter entered.

"Hey, we were wondering when you'd show up," Jürgen greeted him and Rolf started with, "How was…"

"Don't interrupt your work. There's nothing to tell. You were both loaded last night. No hangovers? I couldn't drink that stuff."

Rolf insisted, "Yeah, okay, but what about…"

"The IOUs? Forget it. We'll use them next time as legal tender."

"I don't mean that. How did you make out with Ilse?" and Jürgen added, "Isn't she great?"

"Look, guys, nothing happened. We said good night at her door and I went home. That's it. I mean, she's Pudding's girl, right? How could you even think I'd go to bed with her?"

"Oh, so you didn't? You don't know what you're missing." Jürgen turned back to bundling the rabbit skins.

"And don't worry about Pudding. He knows what's going on," Rolf reassured him. "She's pretty much in the public domain."

"Anyway, I need two bundles rabbit, black. And then show me some seals. This thing with Ilse, let's not talk about it. I am really having some trouble with that."

Walter was busy for the rest of the afternoon packing the goods he had collected and taking the smaller parcels to the post office. In the evening, Martin Geier helped him carry the larger packages to the railway express office and then said good night.

A couple of young men from Niddastrasse stood on line with Walter. "Your boss not in today?" one of them asked with a smirk.

The other fellow grinned. "You have any idea where he is?"

"No, why?"

"Oh, nothing. Probably away on business."

Walter did not pay much attention to their pointed questions, but he remembered Geier once mentioning something about Pinkert being absent for days and that not even his wife knew where he was.

On his way home he allowed himself nothing more than a frankfurter and a Coka Cola for supper. You had an expensive lunch, his conscience told him, just to avoid the remarks and innuendos of your friends. And later you had to face them anyway.

Walter had not seen Pudding since their poker game and the cheap wine the evening before. He still had to clear the air and tell him that Ilse had asked him to come up, but that he had declined.

Rolf Klein, known only as Pudding, perhaps for his wobbly walk or his puffy face, had come from Leipzig when the first fur companies resettled in Frankfurt. That was in the late 1940s. He left behind his aging mother and a pregnant girlfriend. Although he received a regular salary from Arthur Selter, he was always short of money. Whenever it was possible to send a package to the other side of the Iron Curtain, he packed a few goodies for his mother. He also mailed money to his girlfriend and their son, now three or four years old.

"Hi Pudding," Walter called out as he spotted him early the following morning going into the coffee shop. "Time for a muffin and a cup of coffee?"

"Sure." They took their seats at the counter. "What's up?"

"Survived the wine? That was pretty bad stuff the other night, huh? Pudding, listen, I just want to say, nothing happened…"

"I know. Ilse told me. Thanks, but me and her—that's not gonna last. With her everything is temporary. Just be careful, don't fall in love with her. That's not the kind of girl she is."

"Yeah? So, you would be okay with it?"

"Come on. She's been with just about everybody on Niddastrasse. She's not gonna leave you alone." Pudding laughed, "You're like fresh meat."

"Damn, is that what she's like? So pretty, real good looking."

"And sexy. Can't get enough of it." Pudding searched his pockets for some change. "Got something on you? I am fifty pfennigs short."

They left the coffee shop. Pudding said, "So, don't worry. Sooner or later, she's gonna get to you anyway."

Martin Geier was already at work when Walter came in. "Good, you are here. Help me with this. We have to tidy up this place, make it look orderly. Reichenberg is coming today."

The main office of Leo Reichenberg's business was in Vienna, with this branch in Frankfurt. Reichenberg was a rich man, a millionaire several times over. A comical figure of less than average height, rotund, with an egg-shaped bald head sitting on his shoulders, he was a jovial type.

Martin Geier, with Walter's help, did what he could to give the lager an orderly appearance. They stacked furs neatly on the floor, hung bundles nicely spaced from the ceiling.

"Grüss Gott, grüss Gott!" Leo Reichenberg stepped into the lager, greeting Geier in the Austrian fashion. He wore a beige leisure suit with a flowery open shirt. One could think he came to attend a Hawaiian luau. "Where is my lovely Frau Kunze, my one and only Frau Kunze? Ah, there she is."

Matronly Frau Kunze stood in the door to the office, wearing her usual simple housedress. Reichenberg ceremoniously kissed her hand as if she were Viennese royalty. "You make me blush, Herr Reichenberg."

"Nonsense, nonsense." With a theatrical gesture he introduced the two people who had come in after him. "This is Mimi, my secretary. Always by my side. Und der Gustl, my driver."

Mimi was dressed in white, carried a pink purse and wore pink shoes and gloves. A few locks of blonde hair escaped from under her pink hat. She was several hands taller than Leo. Gustl, properly attired in chauffeur uniform, held his cap in his hands. He bowed and smiled awkwardly, obviously used to his boss's antics.

Martin Geier said, "Willkommen to Frankfurt, Herr Reichenberg. May I introduce? This is Herr Walter Hansen. He is Herr Pinkert's new man."

"Pleased to meet you, Herr Reichenberg."

"Ah, Herr Hansen. Yes, yes. Pinkert, Pinkert… Where is my good friend Pinkert? Don't tell me he is on one of his… one of his escapades?" He winked at Frau Kunze. "You know about those things."

"I don't know, Herr Reichenberg. I don't know what you mean, Herr Reichenberg. You are making me blush again, Herr Reichenberg. Really."

"Now, now, Frau Kunze." He motioned her gently back into the office. Mimi went in with them and Martin Geier followed.

Walter, left alone with Gustl, asked, "You drove them all the way from Vienna to Frankfurt? He doesn't like to fly?"

"He has this brand new Mercury. His dream car, he calls it. It's okay, V8, two hundred horsepower, runs well.

Nice piece of machinery. Just took us eight hours yesterday. That's with the border crossing and all."

After a brief chitchat, Walter went into the office to look for the morning mail. Frau Kunze was offering coffee while he sorted through the letters he found in the in-box. There were orders to keep him busy for the rest of the morning and the afternoon.

Wehage's Round Table was crowded, as usual at lunchtime. Pudding and Ilse sat at a table with two young men Walter had met before.

"Pull up a chair, join us," Pudding waved him over. "You know Heinz and Manfred; they're at Westfell."

"Yes, sure." Walter sat down. "Reichenberg's in town. Do you know him?"

"Oh, he's here?" said Manfred. "Did he give you money? He usually hands out twenty-mark bills to the apprentices, especially to the commissionaires."

"He never gave me anything," said Pudding.

"You're not an apprentice. You make enough money," laughed Heinz.

"What do you have to do for twenty marks?" Ilse questioned. "He doesn't get much from me for twenty. Not even a quickie."

"He's a gentleman, Ilse. He's not gonna offer you money."

"Oh, then he must be queer."

"He's not queer," Walter corrected her. "He travels with his own... he calls her his secretary. More like a personal assistant, or something like that. Mimi's her name."

"With his kind of money I'd have my own Mimi too," Heinz chuckled.

"How come he's so rich?" asked Walter. "I don't see Geier doing a lot of business here. All his Persian lamb he shipps to Vienna."

"He does wholesale in Vienna," said Pudding, "but he needs this office here in Frankfurt. Geier is a good man. Keeps his finger on the pulse. He also has someone in London for the big Persian lamb auctions."

"All they've got here is fox. Gris fox, silver fox, white fox and some beaver and nutria," said Walter. "I didn't know he was such big shot."

"I don't care how he makes his money. Come on, let's go and say hello." Heinz urged Manfred to finish his dessert. "You coming with us, Pudding?"

"No, go ahead. I see you later."

Walter finished the beef stew and started on his dessert. "What's this with the money Leo Reichenberg gives away?"

"He's a big show-off, a joke," Ilse said.

"Yeah, he's a bit of that, but he is smart too. After all, his local business depends on the commissionaires, and that's the young people."

"Man, I can use an extra twenty marks. I don't know how I'll make it through September." After buying lunch coupons at Wehage's, Walter was nearly broke. "To change the subject, Pudding, what's all this talk about Pinkert, my boss? He didn't come in yesterday and today he isn't here either. He doesn't tell anybody where he goes. What do you know about this?"

"If I were him, I wouldn't tell anyone either," Ilse blurted out. "He has another fam…"

"Shut up, Ilse," Pudding cut her off. "You don't know that. It's all rumors," and to Walter, "The man has problems. From the war. From time to time his temper flares up. He was wounded, the British took him prisoner. He spent years in England."

"That's rumors too," Ilse defended herself. "Why don't you ask Arthur Selter, he knows. He saw him in London with…"

"Stop that. Selter is a drunk. You know that." Pudding wanted to put an end to it. "Anyway, it's not our business. I happen to like Hans Pinkert. He is a decent man. Something happened to him in the war."

Walter, too, did not want to go on with it. He had no idea that his simple question would open such a sensitive debate. "Yeah, let's drop it. I have work to do. Someone sent in an old muskrat coat. I need some skins to match for repair. I'll come around to see what you have."

Together they left Wehage's and went back to Niddastrasse. On the way, Ilse whispered to Walter, "If Reichenberg gives you twenty marks, maybe we can celebrate. You and me. With a couple of drinks. My place? Tonight?

Chapter Four

Before his departure, Reichenberg had left twenty marks with Frau Kunze for Walter. That gave him a respite of a few days. But then he had bought a bottle of wine to take to Ilse, and the following day he had lunch for his last coupon at Wehage's Round Table. He was broke.

Pudding told him, "Sorry, I just spent my last money on a postage stamp for a birthday card I sent to my boy. He'll be five. Why don't you come in for lunch; somebody will help you out with a coupon."

One evening Frau Kunze gave him five marks to pay a porter for taking two large packages to railway express. Walter made two trips and carried the heavy boxes himself. He survived for another couple of days.

He heard about a cafeteria under the freight station, for railroad workers. "Lunch is one fifty," somebody told him. Walter found his way through an underground maze of passages, with trains shaking the low ceiling above, to a noisy room full of greasy, coal-blackened men eating at long trestle tables. With his last coins in hand, Walter stood on line at the counter for a tray of food, only to learn he needed three marks as deposit for fork, knife and spoon. He had to leave hungry.

Still there were five days left in September, and all he had were those useless IOUs from that poker game a couple of weeks ago. Write to my father, Pinkert had told him. What

41

good would that do? His father would first ask him, What did you do? How could you let that happen? And then, if he sent any money at all, it would come much too late. His boss would not give him another advance; he had made that clear.

Somehow, with change left over at the post office, to be repaid later, and some help from his friends, Walter made it to payday.

"Congratulations!" Pinket said, "Here's your first full pay. What are you going to do with all that money?" He laughed and shook Walter's hand vigorously.

"Thank you, Herr Pinkert." Indeed, for a moment Walter fancied himself a rich man. I have to be prudent here, he told himself. I must never run out of money again.

He paid Frau Kohl seventy-five marks rent for October, bought twenty-five lunch coupons at Wehage's Round Table, repaid some debts and already he was left with less than fifty marks. Sure, he had a place to stay, could have lunch every day, except Sundays, but what about breakfast and dinner? He made his calculations. With extreme caution he would be able to keep himself from starving to death. No Anagnostopolis, no wine from the old man's vat, no movie, no entertainment—nothing.

How did his friends manage? They too had to live on two hundred marks a month. Rolf and Jürgen were apprentices at Interfurs, but they were roommates and shared the rent. Heinz and Manfred, he learned later, lived with their parents. Pudding, who practically ran Arthur Selter's business, probably made five or six hundred a month, but he sent half his income to his girlfriend and their son in Leipzig.

On his daily rounds of the fur wholesalers and manufacturers, Walter made the acquaintance of Herr Samuel Scheiner. In his small shop on the top floor of a building still in dire need for repair, Scheiner employed three young women. On as many sewing machines, they pieced together remnants of Persian lamb and other curled articles to plates, semi-finished products to be sold to furriers. The machines were humming in short bursts; the girls didn't interrupt their work as Walter entered.

Sam Scheiner assumed that Walter knew how to sew. He took him aside. "My girls do terrible work. Look at this plate. See the pattern? It's all wrong. How can I sell this? You come in the evening and fix it. I pay you two marks an hour."

"But Herr Scheiner, I don't…"

"Yes, you will do a better job than these women. You come at six or at seven? When? At six, okay? You take this apart and then sew it back together. The right way."

"Well, Herr Scheiner, I can try."

"Nonsense. I look at you, I see a furrier. You are a furrier, right? You come?"

Walter had watched his father sort the skins, match and cut them. He had also observed the woman working the sewing machine, and even tried it out a couple of times. I know how to insert the thread, he encouraged himself; how to fold the fur, leather side out—all that, but I've never done any real work. So, where did Scheiner get the idea that I could do a better job than his workers?

"All right, Herr Scheiner. I'll see what I can do. But I'm not sure…"

"You work two, three hours, maybe more." He showed him a stack of half finished plates. "Most of them need fixing.

Can I sell as they are? No. I cannot sell." He folded over plate after plate. "See? This here, and that. You come at six?"

Ilse met him as he walked down the stairs, passing the floor where Arthur Selter had his lager. "Hey Walter, going home? There's still half a bottle of wine left. Come with me? We had fun the other day, huh? Talking until midnight... Tonight we could have real fun, know what I mean?" There was her enticing laugh.

"Damn, I wish I could, but not tonight, Ilse. Thanks. Save the wine for some other time. I'm going over to Scheiner, help him with some work. You know him?"

"He the one who buys odd lots and junk? What does he want you for?"

"I don't know. Sewing? He thinks I know how. Anyway, next time, okay?" Damn... But I need the money. Maybe Ilse tomorrow? Scheiner is not going to call me back, once he sees my work. Two marks an hour... That's not gonna happen again.

In anticipation of earning some extra cash, Walter allowed himself a knackwurst and a glass of milk at the coffeehouse and then climbed the stairs to Samuel Scheiner's shop. It was shortly after six and the three machines were idle.

Scheiner greeted him, "Take this machine, or that one. We start on this stack." He piled flawed plates on a table next to the machine Walter had chosen.

In the first hour Walter broke two needles and had to figure out how to replace them. During the next hour he began to understand what Scheiner required him to do and thereafter work seemed to slide into a routine.

After four hours he still did not think his work had improved the quality of the plates, but his boss was obviously convinced of Walter's talent. "You come back tomorrow, maybe one more day, until we finish all of them," and without even inspecting his work he added, "Good job."

By the end of the week, Walter had earned twenty-four marks, an amount that only days before was beyond his dreams.

Beyond his dreams... Once, walking past the café at the Hauptwache, he saw people sitting at small tables, enjoying an aperitif, a cup of coffee or a pastry. I want to do that, he thought then; I want to be able to sit there, read the paper and ask a waiter to bring me a glass of beer, or something in a small glass.

On Sunday, in his suit, the only one he had brought from home, dress shirt and tie, Walter chose a table by the window. He wanted to see who walked by, or perhaps be seen by whoever walked by. He unbuttoned his jacket, crossed his legs, leaned back in his chair and tried to look relaxed in this unaccustomed role.

A couple of hours later, when he left the Hauptwache, he had spent half of his earnings for the three evenings at Scheiner's place. The frankfurter, a tiny slice of bread and two beers cost him more than three lunches at Wehage's.

His Sunday extravaganza did not remain a secret. "You did what? At the Hauptwache? Where the hell did you get the money?"

"Look, Jürgen, I didn't know I could sew. I guess it's in my blood. My father, my grandfather—they were all furriers. So, Scheiner... You know him? He asked me to come and sew some plates. You know, the stuff he does? Those

Persian lamb plates? I had to figure it out and then… I don't know. He didn't even check it out, just told me to come back next day and the next."

"You know how to sew? On those machines? Man, maybe we can go into business ourselves."

"What are you talking about? I didn't come to Frankfurt to sew. I could have done that at my father's shop."

"No, I don't mean that. We could be the ones who sell those odd lots to guys like Scheiner. You know, the junk. For example, the stuff Reichenberg rejects for shipment to Vienna."

"Oh, yeah? And how would we manage that? Even Reichenberg doesn't give anything away for free."

"We talk to Martin Geier. He can give us thirty days credit."

"Scheiner doesn't pay cash either."

"He would, if you give him two percent discount. Ask him."

"First I'll have to talk to Geier. But, look, Jürgen, I don't know how Pinkert would react to me running my own business on the side."

"You see, that's why you need me. My bosses don't care. They sit in London and hardly ever show up here. You just make the connection between Geier and Scheiner, I'll do the rest."

Three weeks later, on an evening after work, Walter and Jürgen dragged, pushed and pulled two huge burlap sacks up the stairs to Samuel Scheiner's loft.

Martin Geier had insisted on selling Reichenberg's odd lot of sub-standard Persian lamb directly to Samuel Scheiner, and agreed with Jürgen and Walter on one per cent commission for them. "Don't tell your boss," Geier said to Walter. "He doesn't have to know about it. Pinkert is… I don't know. He is unpredictable. Better keep it to yourselves. Anyway, I think he is in London again."

At the end of the month, Frau Kunze handed Walter a check for seventy-five marks, made out to Jürgen Springsguth. "Better this way. No conflict of interest," she said confidentially. "Just in case Herr Pinkert finds out."

Jürgen looked at the check and then at Walter. "Leo Reichenberg. You see that? We're doing business with Leo Reichenberg."

He opened an account at the Frankfurter Handelsbank, deposited the check and said to Walter, "That's our funds for future transactions."

"What about Pudding and Horst? Do they know what we are doing?" Walter asked. "And Ilse, does she know?"

"Yeah, that's okay. They don't talk. Now, Heinz and Manfred at Westfell, you know… We're not gonna tell them. The fewer people who know, the better."

From time to time Walter worked in the evenings on plates at Scheiner's shop. At other times he joined the friends at Anagnostopolis or met with them at Pudding's place. Now, that he made some extra money, Walter felt more at ease. Instead of the cheap wine siphoned from the old man's vat, he brought a bottle of Riesling or Spätlese to drink while playing poker and listening to jazz.

"So, Pudding, what's this about my boss, Hans Pinkert? Everybody is so secretive about him. Geier said the other day something, like, he's unpredictable. Frau Kunze acts a little… I don't know. What's going on? Something I should worry about?"

47

"He likes you. Keep it that way. Don't pry. It doesn't concern you."

"Pudding, why don't you tell him what we all know?" Ilse goaded him. "He goes to London to see his…"

"That's all rumors. I don't spread rumors."

"Selter said, he saw him there with a woman and a child. That's no rumor."

"You know Selter is a drunk. When did he say that? Did you sleep with him, too?" Pudding asked jokingly. He and Ilse had recently split up, but there were no hard feelings and Ilse remained one of the group.

"I don't sleep with drunks. They're disgusting."

Walter said, "So, let's say it is true that he has another family in England. Is that really such a big deal? Everybody on Niddastrasse seems to know."

"His wife and Klaus, his son, they don't know," said Ilse. "The wife is always the last to find out," and with that they dropped the subject.

Rolf and Jürgen arrived. Rolf took the cheap wine he had brought out of the bag. "Oh, I see! You don't drink this stuff anymore." He looked at Walter. "Jürgen told me you're swimming in money. I wish I knew how to sew. And that deal you have with Leo Reichenberg… Just don't let Pinkert find out. He has a temper."

"I know. That was a one-time deal," said Walter. "Geier's not going to do it again, so forget about it. "

Walter had brought the old IOU slips and they played poker, listened to some records and drank the cheap stuff first, then the wine Walter had donated.

On their way home, Walter asked Ilse, "Do you really think his wife doesn't know? That he has another woman and a child in London? How can he keep that secret?"

"She will find out sooner or later," and, as they approached her door, "so, are you coming up?"

Walter hesitated for a moment. "Yeah, okay."

One of Ilse's old landladies met them in the hall. "Oh, another nice young man."

Chapter Five

With the first cooler days of autumn, the constructions at Niddastrasse neared their completion. The street received a coat of asphalt and the sidewalks were put in before winter weather would turn the hub of the international fur trade into a muddy swamp.

On Monday morning, as Walter came in, Martin Geier was already at work. He greeted him with a peculiar smile and pointed to the office. "They are waiting for you."

"Ah, Walter. Come in, come in," Pinkert called out. "Meet my son, Klaus." A skinny young man in suit and tie stood beside Frau Kunze. "This is Walter Hansen. He is with me now for... How long, Walter? Since August, that's almost four months."

Arrogance written all over his face, Klaus gave Walter one quick glance. With a blasé smirk, he turned his eyes away as if to say, you're not worth a second look.

Walter reached out to shake hands. Klaus Pinkert seemed reluctant for a second, but then put all his strength into his handshake, trying to imitate his father's firm grip.

"Klaus will be joining the firm," Pinkert announced. "I am sure you will work well together." He slapped his skinny son on the shoulder. "He'll be of great help around here."

51

Oh, God help me! I have to work with this smart ass? Walter swallowed and forced a smile. "I am sure he will," and to avoid further comment they might expect from him, he stepped around the desk and put a hand on Frau Kunze's shoulder. "Morning, Frau Kunze. Any mail yet? What do we have to do today?"

"I didn't open it yet."

"Let's see then." Walter found the letter opener and began to slice open the mail.

"I will take Klaus for a walk around Niddastrasse," said Pinkert. "Introduce him, get him started." Father and son left.

Alone with Frau Kunze, Walter slumped down in a chair. "What do you make of all this, Frau Kunze?"

"Oh, Walter, you will find out soon anyway. You didn't hear this from me, but it's no longer a secret. Herr Pinkert and his wife were divorced last week."

"All the rumors were true, then. Is he going to move to London? Oh, please, don't tell me... Is that why he brought his snotty kid in? How long did you know this?"

"Well, this is not exactly news to me, but Herr Pinkert is so unpredictable. I told you that, remember? And he has a temper."

"But is he moving to London? I'll have to deal with this arrogant bastard? Or will he close down here and I am out of a job?"

"No, no. The way I understand it, he will be moving between London and Frankfurt. His son is to keep an eye on things here. You know, family..."

By noon, the news of Hans Pinkert's divorce and his son joining his firm had spread all over Niddastrasse. The lunch crowd at Wehage's Round Table had a field day.

Walter came in with Ilse, and immediately Heinz and Manfred called them over to their table. From another table, Pudding, Jürgen and Rolf signaled to join them.

Two chairs were free at Heinz and Manfred's table. Ilse nudged Walter toward them. The questions, jokes and innuendos began before they sat down.

Heinz grinned. "You have a new boss, I hear?" and Manfred teased Walter, "You lucky dog!"

Jürgen leaned over from the neighboring table. "I met young Pinkert this morning. What an asshole. Doesn't know a fox from a seal."

"Better show him right from the start that you're the boss," said Pudding.

"You should ask for a raise," said Rolf, "now that you'll have to teach this kid the ropes."

"Listen, I have no idea how this is going to work out. I guess, I'll have to sit down with Pinkert; the father, I mean. He can't put his snotnose son in charge over me. The kid is eighteen, Frau Kunze told me. Just out of school. Pinkert can't just pack up and leave. There's a business to take care of."

"You'll be all right," said Pudding. "Just let the kid know you're the boss."

"That won't be so easy. He's the boss's son. I'll have to walk a fine line, not step on any toes, or I'm out of a job. Pinkert has a temper, you know."

"Here's what you do," said Manfred. "You treat him with respect, as if he knew all about this business, as if he were an expert. Don't teach him anything. He'll fall flat on his face."

Walter thought that was good advice. Let the snotty kid stumble into his own pit. He returned to the lager and found Pinkert and his son standing with Martin Geier at the long table where Geier was sorting Persian lambs. Klaus, trying to look professional in his brand new white smock, observed him with a critical eye.

"See what he is doing, Klaus?" Pinkert asked his son. "Our friend Geier is quite the expert on Persian lamb. You can learn a lot from him." He turned to Walter who just came back from lunch. "Right, Walter?"

"Oh yeah, sure. But Klaus will have no trouble in this business. I can see it already… seems to run in his veins."

Martin Geier made a half turn and looked at Walter to see if he was serious. Klaus had a smirk on his pale face and his father cautioned, "Now, now. We will have to see about that."

Walter faced Klaus. "No, really. You made a good impression on the guys at Interfurs. Jürgen Springsguth told me. I just had lunch with him at Wehage's. You'll do very well." I hope I'm not putting it on too heavy.

"Wehage's? That dump? I hardly think I would want to take my lunch there."

What an arrogant son of a bitch, thought Walter, but he said, "Of course not. I wouldn't suggest it. That's for us apprentices, you know, the newcomers in the business. You on the other hand…"

"It might not be such a bad idea to get to know the young crowd, become friends with them," his father

54

interrupted. "I see, you are already friends with my good man Walter."

How long can I keep up this farce, Walter asked himself. As soon as he meets my friends, he'll find out how they feel about him. They won't treat him gently.

Hans Pinkert broke into his thoughts. "By the way, Walter, I will not be here as much as I would like. Seeing you two getting along so well, Saturday afternoons or on a Sunday, you might do something together. Go to a ball game, see a movie. Introduce him to your friends."

"Dad, I can take care of myself."

"I know. It's just a suggestion." To Walter he said, "You know what I mean. Take him under your wing."

In the days that followed, Klaus Pinkert became less arrogant toward Walter, but still displayed an attitude of exaggerated self-importance. His inflated ego, his obnoxious superiority, was hard to endure.

Walter didn't let his annoyance show. "I know, Wehage's Round Table is far beneath you. I usually eat my lunch there. With my friends, you know. Maybe some day you might want to join us. You met most of them already. Horst Klein—we call him Pudding—from Selter's; Jürgen Springsguth and Rolf Herbert at Interfurs. Did you meet Heinz and Manfred? They are with Westfell."

"My father is going back to London tomorrow. Then maybe I can go with you once. My father, you know, he wouldn't approve of me having lunch at Wehage's."

That, of course, was nonsense. His father had suggested he meet the young men in the business and become friends with them. What was he talking about?

"I understand," said Walter who wondered where this paleface kid got his arrogance. His father wasn't like that. "Sometimes we get together at Pudding's place or at the wine cellar of Anagnostopolis." What am I getting myself into, he thought. They will tear him apart, make minced meat of him.

In the evening, Walter told Ilse, "I am in so much trouble. Pinkert wants me to take his son, this obnoxious kid, around to ball games, the movies and to meet the guys. Have you met him? Has this smirk on his face, like he's better than everybody else."

"I haven't seen him. Better than everybody? I'll find out real quick if he's any good, know what I mean? I'll find out how good he is in…"

"Ilse, stop it. He's eighteen. Pale and skinny."

"All right, all right. If you say so."

"Where's Rolf? Isn't he supposed to bring the wine?" asked Heinz.

"He'll be here. He's picking it up right now," said Jürgen.

They met at Pudding's place to play cards and Walter told them about Klaus Pinkert. "His father wants me to bring him together with us."

"What? He'd be crawling back to his mommy, crying. I couldn't deal with him the way you do." Jürgen laughed. "Is he even old enough to drink?"

"He's eighteen. Manfred, you think I should treat him with respect." Walter shook his head. "I don't know how long I can do that with a straight face."

"Can't we all treat him as if he were a normal guy?" Manfred wanted to end the discussion. "Either he straightens out or he won't last long on Niddastrasse."

"Right. Leave the kid alone," Pudding agreed. "If we are screwing with him and he tells his father, Walter can lose his job."

"Screwing?" Ilse pretended to take literally what Pudding said. "Walter told me not to..." The doorbell interrupted her.

"That's Rolf with the wine." Pudding got up to open the door. "Let's not talk about him any more."

"Well, should I bring him with me next time?" Walter asked.

"Bring whom?" Rolf came in and put two bottles of wine on the table.

"We are talking about Klaus Pinkert," Heinz told him. "Have you met him?"

"The snotty kid with the pale face? Yeah, his father showed him off the other day. What's the matter with that guy?"

Pudding said, "Come on, you want to talk all evening about him or play some cards?" He picked up one of the bottles and looked at the label. "Is this wine any good? Ilse, you know where the corkscrew is. And bring those mugs or jars we always use."

"When will I get to know this paleface snotnose?" she said as she went to the kitchen to get the corkscrew and the mugs. "I haven't had a new guy for weeks. Ah, but Walter told me to leave him alone."

They began to play poker, using the old IOU slips and drank the wine Rolf had bought at a discount store. They all chipped in and then none of them had any money left.

Chapter Six

Walter has not had another sewing job from Samuel Scheiner for some time and the seventy-five marks he and Jürgen Springsguth had earned on that odd lot of Persian lamb from Leo Reichenberg were gone. They had spent it all one crazy night at the *Japan Stube*. Monique and Keiko, the two topless dancers, had promised to go home with them, but by closing time they were nowhere to be found.

Ilse came back from the kitchen. "So, tell me, what happened to you two at the Japan Stube the other night?" she taunted Walter and Jürgen." You didn't tell me anything about that."

"What? You went to the Japan Stube?" asked Heinz. "Where did you get the…"

"We had some money," said Walter, and to Ilse, "nothing happened. Jürgen called them over to our table between their numbers. We had a good time."

"With their breasts hanging out? You must have had a good time," laughed Ilse.

"They put something on. We had a couple of bottles Haute Sauterne. That's all."

"Not exactly," Jürgen added with a big smile. "Monique and Walter were going to take the train to Hamburg together for Christmas. She's from Hamburg."

"Is that true, Walter? You are going home for Christmas? Show a topless dancer off to your parents, but you wouldn't take me?"

"No, I wouldn't have taken her to my parents. Only for the train ride. She would have stayed in Hamburg. But now I'm not going."

"Because she stood you up?" asked Heinz, visibly enjoying the story.

"No, because I don't have the money for the ticket and my father isn't sending any. I was hoping for some work from Scheiner, but I didn't hear from him."

"Hey, can't we all go to the Japan Stube on Christmas Eve?" Ilse asked enthusiastically. "Walter, I let you have your fun with Monique."

"That place is booked weeks in advance," said Jürgen, "but we can try for New Year's."

"Yeah, but that's not cheap. You think Pinkert will give me a bonus for Christmas? It's not even been half a year yet."

"He'll give you something," said Manfred. "Oh, but he will probably be in London. Then you'll get it from his snotnose son." He added seriously, "Make sure you thank him properly."

They all laughed, but Pudding said, "Again with that kid. Come on, deal the cards."

Frau Kunze called Walter into the office and handed him an envelope. "Before he left for London, Herr Pinkert told me to give you this. It's not much, he said, but you've been here only four months." Klaus was standing by with a blasé grin in his face.

Walter counted five ten-mark notes. Can't complain, he thought, and he thanked Frau Kunze.

Klaus surprised him with," My mother and I would like you to come to our house on Christmas day for coffee. Four, four-thirty. See you then." He turned around and went out to the lager. Walter could not reply; he was too flabbergasted.

"What's Frau Pinkert like? Did you ever meet her?" Walter asked Frau Kunze.

"She's okay, I think, but Klaus seems to be taking after her. I met her only a couple of times. Wears a permanent sarcastic smile on her face, like her son, but not without humor. I don't know what to make of her."

"So, what do I do? I have to go, right?"

"Take her a bouquet of flowers. You'll be all right."

Ilse met Walter for lunch at Wehage's. "Want me to go with you?" she asked.

"You're not invited. How can you go with me?" Walter took her seriously. "Flowers, said Frau Kunze. What kind?"

"Get carnations. They're not too expensive. They sell them at the train station."

Walter showed up at the Pinkert residence at four fifteen. Frau Pinkert herself answered the door. He held the unwrapped flowers out for her to take.

"Oh, lovely," she said. "I hope they weren't too expensive. Carnations are cheap these days."

"Thank you for inviting me," said Walter.

Klaus joined them in the hallway. "Take off your coat and hang it here. Carnations, huh? From the train station, I guess. They look like it."

Walter felt like punching him in the nose. What's wrong with the flowers? Not good enough? Frau Pinkert took them to the kitchen and Walter saw no more of them.

Several people were seated around a coffee table in the living room. He did not recognize any of them. There was a Christmas tree in one corner, a grandfather clock in another and gladiolas, roses and tulips on a side table. Should have gotten the tulips, thought Walter, but they were two marks apiece.

"This is Walter Hansen. He is the apprentice in my firm," Klaus introduced him. "My father hired him, now I have to show him the ropes. He's doing very well."

Walter was boiling inside. They seated him at the table, served coffee and cake and continued their small talk, all about their families, their kids, their dogs—no effort was made to include him in the conversation. Why the hell did they ask me to come here? How soon can I leave? Five marks for the flowers, what a waste.

"More coffee?" Frau Pinkert asked, bringing him back from his ruminations.

He saw his chance. "No, thank you. I have to go. I have a party to go to," he lied and stood up. "It was nice meeting you." He nodded and backed out of the room. "I'll talk to you tomorrow," he said to Klaus as he put on his coat. He did not conceal the anger in his voice.

Walking home, Walter did not feel the cold air on this winter evening. "I will make life miserable for this insolent bastard, even if it costs me my job," he mumbled. *His* firm?

His apprentice? Oh, he's got it coming! Wait until Jürgen, Rolf and the others hear about this. They will tear him apart. He won't last on Niddastrasse. They'll make sure of that.

Jürgen Springsguth managed to reserve a table for four at the *Japan Stube* for New Year's Eve. They arrived at the nightclub by ten thirty, paid the cover charge of fifty marks, and the hostess showed them to their table. The place was filled to capacity.

"I make believe I'm with Jürgen," Ilse whispered into Walter's ear. "Then you can have your fun with Monique."

Their table was a good distance from the stage, not at a prime location. "I don't think she's here," said Walter. "That's a different girl." A dancer in a kimono was performing some sort of Japanese dance. "Unless I don't recognize her with all that make-up and the hairdo and..."

"And her breasts tucked away under that kimono," Ilse finished.

"Maybe it is Keiko," said Rolf. "Will she take her clothes off later?"

They ordered a bottle of Haute Sauterne. Ilse asked the waitress, "Is that Keiko or Monique on the stage there?"

"I don't know. I'll ask."

She came with the wine and filled their glasses. "Her name is Rita. Monique and Keiko are no longer here," she told them.

Walter mumbled, "How about that, huh?"

"Yeah, how about that," Jürgen repeated. "Too bad. Anyway, how much money do we have? We have to get at least another bottle."

Rita left the stage to moderate applause. Then a trio of piano, bass and violin played some nostalgic tunes and after that Rita, now in an evening gown and not Japanese at all, came back on stage. The trio played a tango and she summoned a man from a front table to dance. After the first few modest moves, her gown suddenly split down the back and fell to the floor. The crowd roared, as she continued dancing provocatively in the tiniest of bra and panties, and then her partner shed his jacket, ripped his pants off and they ended their number in semi-nudity.

The pair disappeared behind the stage. A few minutes later and fully dressed, they joined a group at the front table.

"Sorry, Walter," said Ilse. "No Monique and no Keiko. And I don't think we can get Rita to come over to us."

"What do you mean? I don't want her."

"Do we have enough money for another bottle?" Jürgen insisted. "It's almost midnight. Should we get a bottle of champagne?" He studied the wine list. "I guess we have to stick with Haute Sauterne."

"Let me see that." Rolf reached across the table for the list. "What are you talking about, there is Asti Spumanti. Come on, how much money do we have?"

They ordered the Asti, and just as the waitress filled their glasses, the piano player hit a few chords in announcement of the approaching midnight hour. In a chorus the guests counted out the last seconds of the old year and then erupted in *"Frohes Neues Jahr!"* Champagne corks popped and confetti dropped from the ceiling.

Walter and Ilse danced in the crowd between the tables. Two young women yanked Rolf and Jürgen from their chairs, spun them around in some kind of a dance.

Gradually relative order returned to the establishment. Half an hour into the New Year, Walter and Ilse made their way back to their table. They fished the confetti out of their glasses. Ilse looked around. "Where are they? Rolf and Jürgen. They didn't leave, did they?"

"There's money under my napkin. Enough for the Spumanti," said Walter.

"They left? Why?"

Someone from the neighboring table leaned over. "They left with the two ladies they were dancing with."

"What do you know? They were dancing? Two ladies? And they left with them?"

"Good for them," said Walter. "Maybe they get lucky."

Walter told his friends that he would bring the snotnose next time they met at Pudding's place. "But we have to be subtle. We can't be too obvious. Remember, my job is on the line. If he tells his father…"

"I feel like beating him up." Rolf had trouble containing himself. "After what he did when you went there on Christmas."

"No," Pudding said. "Walter is right. We can't come on too strong."

Walter tried hard not to let his anger over Klaus's arrogant behavior get the better of him. One evening in early January they walked out of the lager together. "Will you join me and my friends for a friendly game of poker at Pudding's place tonight?" Walter asked him. "You know, to hang out?" He knew this could really turn ugly. Nobody could stand the snotnose, as they now called him. Does this idiot not know that?

"Tonight? You mean now?" Klaus asked as if he had a busy schedule, as if he were going through his mental appointment book. "Ah, a meeting..." He pretended to think aloud. "Ah, that was canceled... Yes, it seems I am free... If your friends don't mind. You know, I am Klaus Pinkert, practically your boss. Will they be comfortable with that?"

"Don't worry about it. Let's go." Walter felt the urge to punch him in the stomach. Keep your cool, he reminded himself. Just a little longer.

Already before Pudding opened the door, they heard Ilse calling out, "The snotnose, the snotnose!" Klaus looked at Walter, quizzically, not knowing what that meant.

"Come on in," said Pudding. "We just opened a bottle. You play poker?"

"You brought any money? We play for high stakes," Rolf hurled at him in a loud voice. "Hundreds! But you're the rich boss, no problem for you, huh?"

"Take off your expensive coat," said Jürgen. "You old enough to drink? Did you meet Ilse? If you're nice she lets you..."

"Cut it out, guys. Ilse, go get him a mug," Pudding interrupted.

"For the snotn..., sorry, for Herr Pinkert? Anything for Herr Pinkert." She got up and squeezed by him in the small room, deliberately brushing her breasts against his arm. "Sit down there, next to me. Never mind them. With me you're safe."

Pudding took Klaus's overcoat and put it on the bed, where other coats and jackets were already piled up. The IOU slips they had issued one drunken night and which they still used for their poker games, lay on the table. Klaus, with a bewildered expression, read the amounts written on them: ten, twenty, twenty-five marks.

Unobtrusively, he fingered his wallet. "I played poker lots of times," he turned to Pudding who, he figured, was the least menacing in this group.

Rolf filled the jar Ilse had brought from the kitchen. "Drink up. We have another bottle."

Klaus took a gingerly sip, made a disapproving face. "Next time, I'll bring a Spätlese. I like a fine wine."

"Yeah, if there is a next time," said Rolf. "Oops, shouldn't have said that," he caught himself, too late. "I'm just kidding." He looked sheepishly at Pudding who was about to say something, but let it go.

Klaus seemed to know a few versions of poker. "What are we betting?"

"Five marks to open. Right, Pudding?" Rolf was bent on fleecing the snotnose.

The doorbell rang. Pudding got up to let Heinz and Manfred in. They each brought another bottle of cheap wine from the discount store.

"Ah, Herr Pinkert Junior has joined us," Manfred said. "I was looking forward to meeting you. I am Manfred, this is Heinz. Pleased to meet you, Herr Pinkert."

"You can call me Klaus." He stood up to shake hands formally.

"Cut out the nonsense, guys," Pudding admonished them. "First names only."

"Even Herr Pinkert?" Ilse asked seriously.

They began to play. "We start with ten pfennigs, as usual," said Pudding. "Enough with the jokes."

Within the hour, they raised the stakes and they resorted to use the IOUs. Only Klaus still put real money on the table. After another hour, and another bottle of wine, Rolf put down his cards and raked in the money and the IOUs. "A pair of sevens beats your kings," he said to Klaus.

Isle who understood nothing of the game, confirmed, "Yes, a pair of sevens…"

"But…" Klaus looked from one to the other.

"That's how we play it here," said Rolf. "You play by our rules or…"

"But I had three kings," Klaus protested. "Surely three kings beat two sevens."

"Not the way we play it here," said Jürgen and nudged Walter under the table. "Right, Walter? That's how we play it here, right?"

Here it comes, the end of my job. Well, so be it. "That's how we play it, my friend. We've had it with you. I told them how you treated me at your house that Christmas day. You, my boss? And I, your apprentice? You showing me the ropes? In front of all those people? You thought you could get away with that? You are the laughing stock on Niddastrasse."

"Yeah, the snotnose, the snotnose!" Ilse chimed.

Rolf said, "We treated you with respect, but you thumbed your nose at us."

Pudding raised his hands. "Hold it, guys. Look, Klaus Pinkert, you had it coming. With your smart-ass attitude, you can't make it on Niddastrase. Walter is right, they laugh at you. Tell your father to send you back to school, but they probably don't like you there either. Take this as a lesson."

Manfred had been quiet during this exchange. Now he said, "I don't think we want to take his money." He reached for the bills and coins on the table in front of Rolf. "Right, guys?" He shoved the pile over to Klaus. "Take it. It's yours."

Klaus took the money and stood up. "Where's my coat? I don't want to spend more time in this company."

"We don't want your snotnose company," said Ilse. "Here, your snotnose coat."

"Ilse, cool it," said Pudding. "We taught him a friendly lesson," and to Klaus who headed for the door, "Next time I see you on Niddastrasse, maybe you'll have a different attitude. Or better, tell your father to find you another job, someplace else."

"Yeah, in Timbuktu!" Rolf spat out as Klaus left the room.

"Oh boy," Walter sighed. "It's all over for me. I am so screwed."

"We will explain it to Hans Pinkert," said Pudding. "I like Hans Pinkert."

After Klaus Pinkert had left, they were quiet for a moment. How much trouble was Walter in?

Pudding said, "Here's what you do, Walter. When he comes in tomorrow morning, you walk up to him and shake his hand. It was all a joke, you tell him. We had a lot to drink. Sure, it got out of hand, things were said we really didn't mean. Sorry, you tell him. And by the time his father comes back from London, or wherever he is, it may all be forgotten."

"That may be okay for you, but I told him a few things, too. The laughing stock on Niddastrasse, and how he and his mother treated me. I brought his mother into this!"

69

"Yeah, and we called him the snotnose," said Ilse.

"How can I get myself out of this?" Walter shook his head. "Besides, he is still the same asshole. I can't stay there. Maybe I should quit before they fire me. Maybe I can get a job with Leo Reichenberg. Hey, maybe I could work for him in Vienna."

"You know what I think?" Manfred leaned toward Walter. "I think he's not even going to tell his father about it. He's too ashamed." He put a hand on Walter's shoulder. "You'll be fine."

"Maybe. But how can I work with this idiot after what happened? Doesn't his father know his son is an idiot?"

"His father has his own troubles, with the divorce, this woman and a kid in London." Pudding always defended Hans Pinkert. "He's not always making the best choices. The war has messed him up, and then prisoner in England."

"That's what I am afraid of. Everyone says he has a bad temper."

"Okay, who will tell me what happened on New Year's Eve at the Japan Stube?" Ilse changed the subject. "You left with two women... What happened?"

"They were both married," said Jürgen. "Their husbands away on jobs or something."

"Or in jail, what do I know?" Rolf added, "But I had a good time."

"How good?" said Ilse, full of expectation.

"Very good. I tell you, very good. I won't say more."

"I had a good time, too," said Jürgen.

"Yeah, but... "

"What are you talking about?" Pudding shuffled the cards. "Are we gonna play or what?"

Walter got up. "I can't play anymore. This thing with Pinkert... What am I going to do? You think we made a big mistake?"

"Don't worry about it," said Manfred. "When's his father coming back?"

"I don't know. Sometimes I think he's not coming back at all, now that he's divorced."

Walter followed Pudding's advice, and the morning after that rough-and-tumble evening, he apologized to Klaus for the bad behavior of his friends. "They are a rough bunch," he told him. "They didn't mean all that, but I'd keep my distance from them for awhile. Know what I mean?"

Klaus responded with a shrug, but said nothing.

Hans Pinkert had been absent for nearly six weeks. He was in a bad mood the day he stormed into the office. Frau Kunze held her hand out to welcome him back, but he ignored her and shook Walter's hand instead, but without a smile.

He leafed through the order confirmations of the past weeks and, without looking up, asked Walter, "Did you take Klaus along on your daily rounds?"

"Yes, Herr Pinkert, we worked well together."

"Did you take him with you, I asked. All he is doing is packing and carrying packages to the post office, he told me."

"He has been doing a lot more, Herr Pinkert. Only the most difficult jobs I did by myself." Walter guessed, Klaus had not told his father about that evening at Pudding's place. Manfred was right; he is too embarrassed.

"How can he learn anything if you don't give him a chance. By the way, he's not coming in today. Got sick over the weekend. Stomach flu or something."

Stomach flu? Thought Walter. Probably just didn't want to be present when his father and I exchanged words. "Sorry to hear that," he said.

The following day, at Wehage's Round Table, Ilse said, "So, Walter, you think he never told his father? You're okay then."

"Yeah—I mean, no. I am sure he didn't tell his father the whole story, but he did complain about me. All he does is pack and carry stuff to the post office, he had told his father. I don't know, but I think Pinkert knows what's going on."

Rolf and Jürgen joined them at their table. Walter repeated what he had just told Ilse. "Pinkert knows something and he's not happy. I didn't let him learn anything, he said, as if it were my fault the kid's an idiot."

"That snotnose," said Ilse.

"Most people I talked to wouldn't even pay attention to him," said Jürgen.

Rolf agreed. "Pinkert should realize that."

"And I have to work with the arrogant son of a bitch. I don't know… It's either him or me. Pinkert no longer likes me, that is clear. Shit, why did this have to happen?"

Jürgen said, "Can you talk to Martin Geier? You are friends with him, right? He knows what's going on. His boss, Reichenberg… Maybe he has a job for you in Vienna. Who knows?"

Leo Reichenberg usually showed up twice a year in Frankfurt. His jovial, comical figure always made quite a stir on

Niddastrasse when he arrived in his chauffeur-driven Mercury—his dream car.

On a warm spring day in April, his driver, der Gustl, dropped him and Mimi off in front of the now fully restored building.

"Grüss Gott, grüss Gott," he greeted first Geier and then Frau Kunze in his exuberant, charming Viennese style. "And how is my lovely Frau Kunze? You look radiant," he exaggerated.

Frau Kunze blushed, straightening the apron she wore over her housedress. "Oh, Herr Reichenberg..."

He shook hands cordially with Walter and then turned to Klaus Pinkert, who waited for someone to introduce him.

Walter said, "This is Klaus Pinkert, Hans Pinkert's son."

"Ah yes, yes. Pinkert, my good friend Hans Pinkert. How are you, young man? Where is your father? Ah, yes, yes. I remember. Unfortunate, unfortunate."

Bleach-blonde Mimi, in a flowery summer dress, pink hat, pink shoes and matching handbag, talked with Frau Kunze and der Gustl stood respectfully aside, twisting his chauffeur's cap in his hands.

Leo Reichenberg and Martin Geier examined a lot of natural sable that just came in from Russia.

"Herr Reichenberg," Martin Geier asked hesitantly and in a low voice, "may I talk to you in private? Perhaps later, when you have a minute?"

PART II
A slender girl with tousled white-blond hair

Chapter Seven

Walter Hansen stood at the corner of Seventh Avenue and Thirty-ninth Street, looking eastward against the direction of traffic. Cars and trucks inched forward, stalled, moved again a few feet, horns blasting. Impatient drivers cursed and made obscene gestures through open car windows. Men hauled and pushed carts with hanging garments, weaving their way through the traffic, between double-parked vehicles and along the sidewalks, shouting at pedestrians to step aside.

Gray eight- and ten-storied warehouse-like buildings lined both sides of the street, separated only here and there by a driveway or a truck entrance. Already the fume-laden air seemed to vibrate in the heat and humidity on this August morning although it was not even nine o'clock. Steam escaped from gully holes, twirled over the asphalt and mingled with the exhaust of overheating cars.

Walter remembered the day—was it three years ago? —when he arrived in Frankfurt on a sweltering morning. But this is different, he told himself. I already have a place to stay, a room of my own, on Manhattan's upper Westside.

The boarding house, run by Mrs. Julia Nieves, actually occupied only one floor in a brownstone on West Eighty-first Street. There were two other boarders: a petite young woman and a middle-aged man. Walter, who spoke English as he had learned it in high school, had great difficulty understanding any of them. Julia Nieves was originally from Cuba, the young woman from Puerto Rico and the middle-aged man from somewhere in the South of the United States, or California; perhaps Boston. Walter was still unfamiliar with the geography and the different accents of this country.

He took a tissue from his pocket and wiped the sweat that had formed under the collar of his white shirt. He had dressed in suit and tie for his interview with Mister Goldsmith. Bernard Goldsmith had an office and small storeroom on street level in the middle of the block. On the glass panel of the door, B. Goldsmith in gold letters curved over the number 720.

A bell clanged as Walter opened the door. To his surprise, the person who came from behind her desk to greet him was not unknown to him.

"Gerda? Gerda Stengel? You here?" he gasped. "You were at Westfell in Frankfurt, if I remember correctly."

"Yes," she laughed. "I heard you were coming. How are you?" They both spoke in German. "Herr Goldsmith said he could use me in New York and I wanted to leave Germany. So, here I am. Over two years already."

"Gerda Stengel… who would have thought. Small world."

"Actually, Gerda Chang. I am married."

Herr Goldsmith came from behind a partition. "Walter Hansen, right?" he said in English. "How is my friend Leo Reichenberg? You came directly from Vienna?"

"Hello, Herr Goldsmith." Walter had hoped Goldsmith would speak German with him, but his English was good enough for uncomplicated conversation. "I want to thank you for letting me come. You and Herr Reichenberg were very kind to make this possible for me. And thank you for arranging my lodging. It is very nice."

Gerda Chang interrupted. "Would you like a 7 Up? I can run across the street to get one from the vendor."

Goldsmith nodded, "Yes, please."

Walter did not know what a 7 Up was and said, "No, thank you."

Bernard Goldsmith sat behind the desk and pointed to a chair for Walter. "So, you want to work in the fur business here. It's not like Frankfurt or Vienna, you know. First, what's your specialty? Persian lamb? Mink? Muskrat? Raccoon? Of course, there is seal and some others, but it's not like Europe. Here everybody is specialized. Someone who knows mink might have no idea about Persian lamb and so on. I don't need anyone, but I can get you in touch with people."

Gerda Chang came back with two dripping cold cans of 7 Up. Walter was so thirsty, his tongue stuck to his palate. *If I had only known what a 7 Up is… Oh, well.*

"It's not easy to get you in," Goldsmith continued. "You have your Green Card, right? You need a Social Security number and then there is the Union."

Walter had a temporary Green Card, thanks to the affidavit Mister Goldsmith had provided for him, but he had no idea what a Social Security number was and what the Union had to do with anything. Not to appear ignorant, he didn't ask. *How they are enjoying their 7 Up,* he thought enviously. *I wonder what it tastes like.* "I will have to find out all about that," he said. "What are my chances, Mister Goldsmith, to find a job?"

"Thorer & Hollender, Interfurs—they all have their branches here in the Garment District. Let me make a quick call."

Gerda Chang and Walter talked for a while about Frankfurt and people they knew, where they were now, what happened to them, while Mister Goldsmith talked on the telephone. When he hung up, he told Walter to go across the street to see so and so at Thorer & Hollender. "They might be able to help you."

During the two years Walter worked for Leo Reichenberg in Vienna, he had met Bernard Goldsmith twice. As it turned out, Goldsmith remembered Walter's father from before the war. "He bought furs from me. I had coffee with your parents at their home in Rendsburg," he reminisced. "You were three or four then." His voice became small and soft as he seemed to turn inwards. "Nice people, your parents." Quickly he added, "But in '38 I had to disappear, you know."

Leo Reichenberg and Bernard Goldsmith had been hiding in mountain villages outside Vienna since the Nazis annexed Austria until the liberation in 1945. Goldsmith took up residence in the United States. Reichenberg remained in Austria and, with the revival of the post-war economy, expanded his business into a multi-million dollar import and export enterprise.

When Walter met Herr Goldsmith for the second time, he casually raised the question of coming to New York. "I don't like it so much here in Vienna. Mountains everywhere, I miss the ocean," he complained. Really, it was more the soft Viennese character, the coffeehouse mentality, the sugary music, the silky dialect he disliked. Goldsmith and

Reichenberg, who was always helpful toward the younger generation, worked out the details for Walter's emigration to America.

After his interview with the manager at Thorer & Hollender, Walter went to talk to the Union boss who had an office down the block. Then he returned to Goldsmith.

"At Thorer & Hollender they told me I had to be in the Union before they could employ me, but the Union boss said, first I had to have a job to become a member. What can I do?"

"Yeah, that's a problem in this industry. You might have to look outside the Garment District."

"You mean, there is fur business elsewhere? Where I wouldn't have to join a Union?"

"No. I mean outside the fur business. Forget the furs."

Walter was confused. "What? I don't understand."

Gerda interjected, "Walter, the German Consulate has a free employment referral service. I know people who found jobs through them."

"That's what I'm talking about. Forget the furs," Goldsmith repeated.

Walter looked at Gerda, then back to Mister Goldsmith. He was perplexed. "My father is a furrier, so were my grandfathers on both sides. After the war I went back to school and then, three years ago, I started in Frankfurt. Furs is all I know. I have never even thought about anything else." For him there was nothing else.

"Well, you might have to adjust your thinking. Gerda, you have the address of the German Consulate?" He leaned forward in his chair. "Young man, there are other opportunities. Get out of this business. Some day you'll thank me for telling you this."

"Think it over, Walter," said Gerda later as they were having a sandwich in a coffee shop on Seventh Avenue. "Mister Goldsmith is right. It's difficult to break into the business here. Maybe impossible."

Walter ordered a 7 Up, but it was served in a glass— water-clear with bubbles and ice. "Is this the same as you had this morning in the office?" he asked Gerda and admitted he had never heard of 7 Up.

"Yes. Listen, you have to get used to a lot of things. I had it easy. I moved in with a girlfriend of mine in New Jersey. At a party I met Joe. Six months later I married him."

"Chang... Is he Chinese, your husband?"

"He is American. His parents came from China. Joe is a chemist at Bristol-Myers in New Brunswick. That's where we live, in New Jersey."

"That's another state, right? Sounds complicated." So many new impressions cluttered Walter's brain. "I am glad I can speak German with you. Yesterday at the Chock-full o'Nuts I asked for a hamburger. 'Mustard, Ketchup, *Maynaise?*' the waitress yelled at me. I didn't know what she wanted, so I said no. Like with the 7 Up. I have so much to learn."

Gerda laughed. "It's only your second day in this country. You're doing great. Listen, I have to go back to work. Take it easy this afternoon. Tomorrow morning go to the Consulate on Park Avenue and Fifty-seventh. They'll give you a list. Let me know how you make out." She rummaged in her purse for some money.

"No, let me..." said Walter and put a five-dollar bill on the counter.

"Uh uh, you don't have a job yet. You can pay after your first paycheck."

Walter had arrived in New York after five days at sea on board the *Berlin* with just over two hundred dollars in his pocket." Thanks," he said. "How long do you think I can live on two hundred? I pay Frau Nieves thirty dollars a week. She gives me breakfast. Toast and an egg in the morning. I have to find a job soon. Washing dishes, cleaning toilets... I don't know what I can do. I have never worked at anything but furs."

"You'll find something. I have to run. Go to the Consulate first thing in the morning. Let me know how it goes."

They said good-bye and Gerda hurried back to her office. Walter was still confused about a future that did not involve furs, but Gerda Stengel had calmed his anxiety. He decided to have a look at what's important in New York: the Empire State Building, the Chrysler Building, the Statue of Liberty, Central Park. He had seen pictures, of course, but he was excited about actually being in Manhattan. He ventured down into the subway, a new world for him, and studied the enormous map with red, blue, green and yellow lines. He found Brooklyn, Queens and The Bronx. He discovered what tokens are and that they cost only fifteen cents. He bought ten of them.

The ride south to Battery Park was an exhilarating adventure. He emerged from underground and breathed the fresher air coming over the bay. And there, small in the

81

distance, smaller than he had expected, the Statue of Liberty. Big deal, he thought, and turned around to see the imposing buildings lining Battery Park. Everything is big here, he thought, even the ferries going across to Staten Island, but the Statue of Liberty is so small. Must be the distance, he thought. Then, slowly coming down the Hudson, the *Berlin*, his home for five days. There she goes, back to where I came from.

A great loneliness overcame him as he watched the ship glide out into the bay, past the Statue of Liberty, on her way to Bremerhaven. In five days I could have been back there and all this would be a dream.

The moment passed. Back underground on a speeding train that took him Uptown, he consulted the map over the door. Lexington Avenue Line, it said there. Now, this is new: that's on the Eastside. He got off at Forty-second Street. Climbing the stairs, found himself in a huge hall: Grand Central Station. Another landmark, but where are the trains? Is everything here hidden away underground? Then, outside again, he discovered the Chrysler Building, too close to see the art deco top he had seen on postcards and in brochures. He walked south on Lexington Avenue, looking back every few steps until he saw the beautiful arched crown and the pointed needle piercing the clouds. At the corner of Thirty-fourth Street, finally the Empire State Building. From there he could compare the two tallest buildings of New York City: looking north, the Chrysler Building, and to the west the Empire State Building. He decided the Chrysler was definitely his favorite.

Walter learned all this Uptown, Downtown, Midtown. The Eastside, the Westside. Buses, taxis, trucks and cars—and people, people, people. Had I not been in big cities like Frankfurt and Vienna before, this would have come as a shock, he reflected. But I am seasoned. I will make New York my home.

Walking along Fifth Avenue, past the Library, past all the fashionable stores, he came to Central Park South and, at the Plaza Hotel, turned west toward Columbus Circle. His long walk in the afternoon heat had tired him, but he did not want to spend another of his precious tokens and continued on foot along Broadway all the way to West Eighty-first Street.

"Got your Social Security card yet?" asked Frank, Julia Nieves's middle-aged boarder. "Can't do anything without it. It shows you are a legal resident. Nobody will employ you if you don't have one."

Again that Social Security card. Bernard Goldsmith had mentioned it. "What's a Social Security card?" Walter asked. They sat at the counter at Lambston's, having a grilled ham and cheese sandwich. Frank drank coffee; Walter had a root beer and was surprised that it had nothing to do with beer. "Tastes like toothpaste," he said. Tired and thirsty after his long walk through Midtown, he would have liked nothing more than a beer. "Why do I need a Social Security card? I have a Green Card, a temporary one at least. That shows I am legal."

"Believe me, you need it. There's a Social Security office a couple of blocks down on Broadway. Bring your passport and Green Card. Prepare yourself for a long wait. Always a crowd in there."

"Tomorrow morning I'll go to the German Consulate. To find a job."

"First thing they'll ask you, Do you haben eine Social Security Karte?" He laughed. "Mein Deutsch is not so good."

Frank, a clerk in a law firm, should know, thought Walter. But the job is most important. I'll do that first, as Gerda told me. "Okay, I'll go tomorrow," he told Frank.

"You met Nilda? What do you think of her? Nice, huh?"

"Who is Nilda?"

"Nilda. At Mrs. Nieves. You didn't see her? She came in as we left and nodded hello. I like her, but she doesn't even see me. A bit younger than me. You should ask her out. She works at a doctor's office. Or a dentist."

"Frank, I need a job before I can ask anyone out." He thought for a moment. "Nilda, huh? Yes, I saw her. She's what, thirty-two, thirty-five? I am twenty-four."

"That's okay. I haven't seen her with anyone." He got up. "I want to catch a movie. You coming?"

"Some other time, Frank. Thanks."

Walter went home and started on a letter to his parents. After the first few lines of *"How are you? I am okay,"* he paused. I really have nothing to tell yet. As long as I don't have a job, what could I say? My father would just bark, Nothing about work? What's he doing? or something like that, and my mother would calm him down, But he just got there.

Then he wrote, *"The trip was fine, the Berlin is a fine ship, New York is a big city, the weather is hot, I walked all day, Bernard Goldsmith sends regards."* He put the pen down. I'll finish that when I have a job.

Mrs. Nieves put a plate with toast and a soft-boiled egg in front of him, and a cup of coffee. "Good morning, Mister Hansen. Job hunting today? Good luck!"

"Thanks. What's the best way to Park Avenue? That's where the German Consulate is. Through Central Park? A long walk, isn't it?"

"No no, don't do that. Never walk through the park. Uh uh. That's where people get robbed and killed. There's a cross-town-bus. It runs from West End Avenue all the way through Central Park to East End Avenue. Get on at the corner of Seventy-ninth and Broadway."

"Really? Well thanks, Mrs. Nieves." Walter finished his breakfast and went out. People get killed in Central Park?

Nilda came into the room. Walter held the door for her. She showed a minuscule smile, then greeted Mrs. Nieves. "Buenas dias, Señora," she said and something like "como está." Just like Frank told me last night. She didn't look at me either. He headed for the bus stop.

The bus was not crowded. Walter slipped his token in the machine next to the driver and took a window seat. After a few stops, the bus entered Central Park, followed the long, winding road and eventually came out at Fifth Avenue. He had seen no people in the park; so, who would get killed there, and by whom?

Walter stepped off at Park Avenue, looked across the wide, divided street and spotted the light gray building with the German flag over the entrance. It was just past nine o'clock. Men in business suits and women in smart attire hurried on their way to work—New York in motion.

On the directory board in the lobby, he found the floor on which the German Consulate General was located. The elevator whisked him up.

The young woman at the reception spoke German. "May I help you?"

"Yes. Good morning. I arrived from Germany a few days ago and I am looking for work. I heard you have a referral service?"

"Ah, for that you will have to go downtown. It's on Broadway." She wrote an address on a slip of paper. "Bring your passport, Green Card and Social Security card. You have your Green Card yet?"

"A temporary one. I don't have a Social Security card yet, but I know where to get one. My Green Card is only temporary."

"What's your name? I'll see if it has arrived already. It might be in your file. Usually takes no more than a month from application. When did you apply?"

"Oh, about eight weeks ago, at the American Consulate in Frankfurt. My name is Walter Hansen."

"Just a moment." She went through a glass door with a sign Archive and returned just minutes later with a folder in her hand. "Now let's see. Oh, here it is. You have your passport and the temporary? I need that."

Walter was prepared and handed her the documents. He had not expected his Green Card so promptly. In Frankfurt they had told him it might take up to six months. Now he was surprised at both the German and American efficiency.

"Sign here and put the date down. I keep the temporary. Here is your passport and the address for the employment office. Welcome to America, and good luck."

"Thank you and auf Wiedersehn," said Walter. On his ride down to street level he fingered the most important Green Card, laminated in shiny plastic, and hummed contentedly to himself. *Now I am really here. A good reason to celebrate. But wait: I don't have a job yet.* His euphoria dimmed just a little.

Damned Social Security card. If I only knew what that's good for.

On the bus back to the Westside, Walter did not let his enthusiasm evaporate and decided to go straight to the Social Security office.

Indeed, there was a crowd of at least thirty-five people, sitting on rows of chairs in a large hall. Women, some pregnant, others with small children, and men of all description, ages and colors. A number was called, and Walter realized he had to have a number. He withdrew a slip from a dispenser. Like in a bakery back home, he thought, and took a seat. Another number was called, followed by a long wait for the next one. A look at his slip told him it would be an hour or an hour and a half for his turn. Ceiling fans stirred the hot, humid air.

Several clerks behind a long counter along the back wall attended to those seeking advice or explanations of their concerns in an unhurried way. They got up to refill their coffee mugs, laughed and chatted among themselves, seemingly unaware of time or the crowd waiting to be called up.

Then it was lunchtime. Three of the clerks left their place; the interval between numbers doubled. When they returned, others left. Walter recalculated his waiting time to three hours, but then numbers were called in short succession. "One twenty-two." He got up. "Here," he called out.

"What you need, honey?" the bosomy woman asked him as he took his seat at her station.

The casual approach took him by surprise. In his mind, he compared the German professionalism with the lax way of doing business here. "A Social Security card," he said. "I am new in this country, just came from Germany. Everybody tells me I need a Social Security card to find work."

"You sure do, honey," she laughed and looked to the left and right for approval from her fellow clerks. "Germany, huh? Now, what can you show me that'll tell me who you are, that you are a legitimate resident and that you ain't no crook." Again she laughed. "Got somethin' to identify yourself, like a birth certificate, a passport, or a Green Card?"

"I have a Green Card," Walter said proudly. "Just got it."

"Good, honey. But then I need to see your passport, too. To make sure, you know. You did bring your passport, I hope," she laughed.

Then, with his passport and Green Card in hand, she told him, "Wait here, honey. Be right back," and walked to a back room. She was gone for a long time.

When at last she reappeared, she had a sheet of paper with a small card stapled to it. She pushed it across the table toward Walter. "These are your instructions and this is the card, in duplicate. Now, I need you to sign here. That's for me. Then you sign here, and both of them cards. One you carry with you at all times, the other you keep in a safe place. Okay? Got that? Good. Now you're on your way. Good luck, honey." She called the next number.

When he came out of the Social Security office, it was nearly three o'clock. Feeling dizzy from hunger and thirst, and the stifling New York heat and humidity, he had a quick hot dog at a street corner, and a Coca Cola.

The train he boarded for his ride downtown was not crowded. The receptionist at the consulate had told him to get off at Fourteenth Street. He found the address easily. A plaque read: German Consulate General, Employment Office. The small room contained a couple of file cabinets; a man and a woman sat idly behind their desks. They seemed happy that someone came to see them.

"Hello! Looking for work? Maybe we can help you. I am Gerd."

The woman added, "You just arrived from Germany? We can assist only new arrivals, for their first job." They both spoke German.

Walter introduced himself. "Here is my Green Card and Social Security card."

"We don't need that. Just your passport. That tells us who you are and when you arrived in the United States." Gerd found the stamp in the passport. "Oh, that's just last Sunday. Ingrid, you have the latest list?" he turned to the woman. "The one with Automotive Imports and Distribution, the Long Island firm?" He looked back at Walter. "They are looking for an inventory clerk."

Ingrid pushed the list across her desk. "There are five companies, all German. The Automotive is on top. Then you have the German Bakery; the German Moving and Storage, they are in New Jersey; German Dry Cleaners up on Eighty-sixth Street; and a food importer, Bavarian Specialties."

"I would go to Long Island first; they seem to be in a hurry," said the Gerd. "But you need to speak some English."

"Oh, I speak English. But, Long Island? How do I get there? It's not in New York?" He scanned the rest of the list. Bakery, storage, dry cleaner's. New Jersey…

Ingrid corrected her coworker. "Gerd, it's not Long Island." To Walter she said, "They are in Queens, Long Island

City, just ten minutes from Grand Central on the Flushing Line. Crescent Street. Get off at Queensboro Plaza. Here, you can have this subway map. It shows all the lines. On the other side are the bus lines."

"Long Island City. Yes, go there first," said Gerd. "It's your best shot. Ah, three thirty already. You go tomorrow morning? Yes? I'll give them a call that you are coming, okay? Walter Hansen, right?"

"Yes. Okay, thank you." Walter turned to leave. "Queens... Is that New York?"

Ingrid called after him, "Yes, and if that doesn't work out, try one of the others. They are all good German companies. Good luck!"

Once outside, and around a corner, Walter found a pub. Flashing neon signs advertised Miller High Life and Budweiser. He entered, sat at the bar and ordered a Budweiser. His first beer in America—ice cold and without a head of foam on top. He had heard of the uncivilized way they drank beer here. He was thirsty and wanted to try it. He drank defiantly, but eagerly to quench his thirst. Something else to get used to.

In the morning, Walter studied the subway map spread out beside his plate of toast and scrambled egg. His coffee got cold while he tried to figure out how to get to Queens.

Frank came in, greeted Mrs. Nieves and sat down opposite Walter. "What you got there?"

"I have to go to Queens for a job. You know where Crescent Street is?"

"No." With a nod he thanked Mrs. Nieves who brought him his coffee, toast and egg. "Long Island City, I guess. Take the number seven train, the Flushing Line."

"Yes. Queensboro Plaza, they told me."

"Oh, now I know where that is." Between bites of his toast and egg he asked, "Did you get your Social Security card? If not, don't even bother to go to Queens. Get the card first," he said emphatically.

Walter smiled in triumph. "I have the card. I have more than that. I also have my Green Card, the permanent one. And I have a whole list of jobs."

"Boy, you have been busy."

Nilda came in. Her lips formed something like "Good morning," then she joined Mrs. Nieves at the kitchen door to talk.

"What did I tell you," Frank whispered across the table. "She's not talking to us."

"Could be she is shy."

Chapter Eight

Ernst Straub spoke German in the dialect that reminded Walter of his time in Frankfurt. He greeted him huskily. "You are Walter Hansen? They called yesterday. You know anything about keeping inventory? We have thousands of items. Nuts and bolts and springs and screws, washers and gaskets. Batteries, cables, spark plugs and so on and so on. Engine blocks, pistons, transmissions. Everything for every make and model of German cars and trucks."

"I was a lagerist in Frankfurt and Vienna," said Walter when there was a pause in Straub's diatribe. He did not have the chance to elaborate that *lagerist* was the term used in the fur business for one who worked in a lager, a fur loft.

"Lagerist? That's what we need here. Only here we call it inventory clerk. This is Paul Kempowski; he's the supervisor. You'll work with him. I am the manager. You call me Mister Straub, I call you Walter." He rattled on like a drill sergeant.

The young man sitting at a row of file cabinets with hundreds of trays sliding in and out of slots grinned sympathetically, or mischievously; Walter wasn't sure. Paul did not interrupt his work, pulling out trays, flipping cards inserted in them, making hasty notes and rolling on his chair on to other trays—all at a speed that left Walter flabbergasted.

93

Mister Straub led Walter through a door out into the storage area. Rows of orderly arranged shelves, some reaching to the ceiling, filled the vast warehouse, which he called the *lager* in German. Hence the confusion to Walter's benefit.

"Parts and accessories," Straub explained. "All by number and by sizes in the same order as the inventory cards in those trays Paul is working on. Come on, follow me to the office."

Walter had a hard time keeping up with him. They went through the inventory control room to the main office and into a cubicle with two desks. A slender girl with tousled white-blond hair stood up and smiled invitingly at Walter.

"You must be Walter Hansen. I am Roswita Peschel." She reminded Walter immediately of Ilse, his girlfriend in Frankfurt. How strange, he thought. Ilse was brunette and petite; Roswita is blonde, tall and slender. Ah, it must be the accent.

"Pleased to meet you." They shook hands. "You must be from Saxony?"

"Leipzig," she laughed. She pronounced it Leipzch. "Where are you from?"

"Oh, Rendsburg. That's in…"

"I know where it is." She had such a friendly, amusing face. Her flowery summer dress was so light, it was almost transparent.

"I lived in Frankfurt and in Vienna for three years."

Ernst Straub interrupted. "Let's get to work here. Enough of that talking. This is a business, not a *kaffeeklatsch*. Roswita, take his information and then get over to Personnel. This is Thursday, so you start on Monday." He strode out, back to the inventory control room.

There had been no question of Walter's qualification for the job; his being a lagerist sufficed.

Walter had found the location easily. Automotive Imports & Distribution, Inc., here known as AID, occupied an entire block on Crescent Street. The main entrance to the pale-yellow, sprawling, one-storied building was at one corner. Trucks entered the wide parking lot from the side street, where the loading platform took up the full length of the rear of the building.

From the moment he met Ernst Straub, Walter had the impression that this man would be extremely demanding, accepting no excuses for mistakes or sloppy work. Praise would never come to his lips. He would be uncompromising but fair.

The Personnel manager gathered Walter's data, of which his Social Security number was of major importance. Without discussion or negotiation, he told him, "Your salary is sixty-five dollars a week. That's gross. We take out the taxes. Payday is every other Friday. After three months you will be enrolled in our insurance plan." He took a breath and continued. "Your job description is Inventory Control Clerk. Straub is your manager, Paul your supervisor. The hours are from nine to five, Monday to Friday. The first year you get no vacation, second year five days. Then every year one additional day. From five years on, ten days. Is that all clear?"

Walter nodded.

"Now, sixty-five dollars is better than what most companies pay. We believe in long-term employment. Once a year your supervisor evaluates your work. Raises are based on merit. The first three months you are on probation. Clear?

Misconduct can get you fired without a warning. Okay? You start on Monday." He stood up to shake Walter's hand. "Welcome to AID." He sat back down and said no more.

Roswita, who had been standing in the background, tapped Walter on the shoulder. "Let's go."

"Thank you, sir," said Walter. He followed Roswita out the door.

They found Mister Straub at his desk in his cubicle. "Monday morning nine o'clock. Be early, not a minute late. We start working at nine," he stressed working, "not coming in at nine, hanging up your jacket, talking, going for coffee. None of that. Paul will show you." He continued with what he was doing.

Roswita's eyes twinkled. "Bye," she said, gave him a small wave and sat down at her desk. Straub looked up briefly, but said nothing.

Walter left the building through the main door where he had come in. He would have liked to talk to Paul about the job he was facing, about Mister Straub and what kind of a boss he was, and about Roswita who he guessed was twenty-two, twenty-three. I will find out soon enough. But there's Friday and the weekend in between. I am anxious to start working— and to see Roswita; just to talk, I mean. And to find out…

As far as he had explored Crescent Street, Walter saw warehouses and small workshops, an auto repair shop and a gas station. At the end of the block opposite AID, there was a multi-storied apartment building, a diner at the corner.

He walked back to Queensboro Plaza, less than five minutes. The subway, here elevated above the rooftops of adjacent buildings, was still called the subway. Strange, thought Walter, but everything is strange, so strange. So much to get used to.

On the train he reviewed in his mind the job interview. So weird, so easy. No questions about previous employments, about his background. All seemed to be settled the instance he walked through the door. *Lagerist*—that was the key word. Straub had heard what he wanted to hear. If only he knew! I hardly know the difference between a nut and a screw, a bolt and a piston.

Then he tried to calculate how he would manage on sixty-five dollars a week. Not too bad, he thought, forgetting about the taxes taken out of his paycheck. Thirty for Mrs. Nieves would leave him with thirty-five dollars, five dollars a day. Once he saw Nilda eating dinner with Mrs. Nieves. He thought, if I gave her five dollars extra, maybe she would me give dinner, too.

It dawned on him that he would not have a single penny to spend on any luxury, a movie or even a beer. It would be like the first months in Frankfurt all over again. There he had made friends quickly. They all had the same problem of money shortage, but they helped each other along. Walter had found ways of scrounging extra cash, working for Sam Scheiner, selling scrap fur products. In New York he saw no such possibilities.

He got off the train at Times Square and walked to Thirty-ninth Street. He needed to talk to someone.

"How did you make out? Did you go to the Consulate?"

"Hi Gerda. Yes, yesterday. My Green Card had already arrived. Then I got my Social Security card and went to the employment office."

"Oh, good. What did they tell you?"

"I already have a job. Just came back from the interview. It's in Long Island City." He pulled up a chair and sat down. "Ever heard of Automotive Imports and Distribution? They call it AID. They hired me right away, just like that."

"Congratulations! All that in your first week. AID? Never heard of it."

"It's automotive parts. No idea. But I want to thank you and Mister Goldsmith. I wouldn't have known what to do. Is he in?"

"He's not here. Preparing for a trip to London and Frankfurt. He leaves tomorrow. So, tell me about this job."

"My boss, Ernst Straub, he's like a drill sergeant in the army. Very demanding. It will be hard to work for him, but I think he is okay. I start on Monday."

"A drill sergeant, huh?

"Well, yes, but that's okay, I think. Remember, I worked for Hans Pinkert in Frankfurt? He wasn't easy to work for either. Had a bad temper."

"Pinkert. Didn't he move to London?"

"Yes. That's why I ended up with Leo Reichenberg in Vienna. I'll tell you about that some other time. What I wanted to ask you: AID, they'll pay me sixty-five dollars a week. Can I live on that?"

"Sixty-five? Before taxes? You can get by, if you're careful. Listen, I spoke to Joe, my husband. We want you to come over next weekend. After your first week of work."

That evening Walter took out the letter to his parents he had started two days before. He sat for a moment, staring at it, then wrote, "Today I had a job interview. I will start working on Monday." He wasn't sure if he should tell them that it had nothing to do with furs. His father would not understand. Later, he thought, some other time, and put the letter back into the drawer of the bureau.

He heard Mrs. Nieves and Nilda talking in the living room. Walter came out of his room and found the two women sitting at the dining table. "Good evening," he said, "I hope I am not interrupting, just want to tell you, I already have a job."

"Congratulations, Mister Hansen," said Mrs. Nieves.

"Thank you, but they don't pay very much. I was wondering... Would you, if I paid you something extra... You know, eating out is rather expensive."

"Mister Hansen, our arrangement was room and breakfast. Let's leave it at that. Did you meet Miss Ponce? Nilda, this is Mister Walter Hansen."

"Nice meeting you," both Walter and Nilda said.

"You will be welcome to have dinner with us sometimes, when there is enough. I ask Miss Ponce occasionally."

"Thank you, Mrs. Nieves. I am willing to pay..."

"No, no. That's not necessary."

On Monday morning, Walter arrived at AID ten minutes before nine. He entered through the side door that led directly from the truck entrance to the inventory control room. Paul Kempowski was already there, just hanging up his jacket.

"Good morning," Walter greeted him.

Paul answered, "Guten Morgen."

Walter had not known that Paul, too, spoke German; the day he first met him, Paul hadn't said a word. "Does everyone here speak German?"

"Not everyone. Top management, Mister Straub and I, one or two on the lager and a few of the technicians. Oh, and Roswita. But we generally speak English here."

The mention of Roswita made him quiver just a little. What's she like, he wanted to know, but instead asked, "Mister Straub, what's he like?"

"Rough on the outside, but... Shhh, here he comes. I'll show you what we do here. At first it seems complicated, but you'll get it."

"Ah, you're here. Good. Paul, you're in charge." Straub stormed out as quickly as he had come in.

The first order sheets came through a window that communicated with the main office, and landed in a basket marked IN. Paul picked them up. "This is what we work with." He pointed to the items on the first order. "Product name, catalogue number, quantity. Look it up on the cards." Sitting on his chair, he propelled himself to the far end of the row of cabinets, pulled out a tray, flipped through the cards. "Quarter inch bolt. They want five. See here: fifteen in stock. Subtract. Write five in this column on the order. Next one." He went down the list of items. "Take that chair, sit next to me. And take off your jacket. Can't work with a jacket."

"How do you find the items among the hundreds, thousands in those trays, and so fast? You know exactly where to look."

"Practice. By the six-digit product number you know whether it's Mercedes, BMW, Volkswagen or whatever, and what type. Truck numbers all start with nine." He put the finished order in a basket marked OUT. "You take the next one. See this? The numbers all start with four and five. That's VW. They want wiper blades and arms, connecting hoses and a pump. Here, use a sharp pencil."

Paul showed him where to look. Walter's chair rolled easily on the smooth floor and he slithered to the center of the row of cabinets. After pulling out half a dozen trays, he found the first two numbers: wiper blades and arms. Then he located the hoses and finally the pump. Paul watched him subtract the items on the inventory cards and make the notations on the order sheet.

Walter felt the need for a rest, but orders kept coming through the window. Paul worked through them like a machine and finished five or more, while Walter struggled with one. Engineers or technicians from time to time interrupted to check on the availability of an item. They liked to stay and talk for a moment, but in this room there was no time for chitchat.

The inventory control room, although air conditioned, was not as cool as the rest of the offices due to frequent opening of the door to the warehouse, exposing them to the hot outside air. The workers came in to pick up completed orders and then carelessly often left the door open.

Ernst Straub came a couple of times to give Paul an instruction or ask him a question. He ignored Walter.

At long last: lunch break. "Where do you go for lunch, Paul? Is the diner across the street any good? Not too expensive?"

"Most days I bring a brown bag. My wife packs a sandwich and an apple or a banana. There is a coke machine in the lager. It's free. Coke, 7 Up, Sprite."

"Well, I'm not married. I guess I'll try the diner."

"Forty-five minutes. Later we have a fifteen-minute coffee break."

So far, Walter had learned nothing about Paul, except that he was married. There just was no time. He also knew nothing about Ernst Straub. And Roswita? He had not seen her in the morning and wondered where she might go on her lunch break.

The hamburger he ate at the diner came with a slice of cheese, and a pickle on the side. Seventy-five cents and a dime tip—not too bad, he thought. Back at the office, he had a free Sprite, another novelty for him. Could have been a 7 Up. Tastes the same.

Paul was talking with one of the workers in the warehouse. They spoke German. "This is Franz. They call him Frank here."

"Walter Hansen." They shook hands. "Where are you from, Frank?"

"I'm from Stuttgart," he pronounced it Sturgatt. "That's where Straub is from. He knew my father."

Walter told them he was from Rendsburg and that he had lived in Frankfurt and Vienna. "Paul, you're from North Germany, too, right?"

"Königberg. Now it's called Kaliningrad. We left in forty-four before the Russians came in. I was a kid then. I grew up in Hamburg." He looked at his watch. "Time to get back in there." On their way back to the inventory control room, he said, "This is my third year with AID."

More orders had come in during the lunch break and Paul said they all had to be processed. "What comes through that window by three o'clock must be out in the lager for shipment by four. Everything that comes in later is for shipment next day. But sometimes, when we're not so busy, they still get it out same day."

Walter was able to finish a few orders before the coffee break and the rest of the afternoon went by quickly. Roswita stuck her head in briefly to give Paul a message from Mister Straub. "Hi, Walter. Doing all right?" she said in her funny Saxon dialect.

"I'm okay, Roswita. How are you doing?" was all he had time to say.

Paul pushed an order over to him. "You finish this one. All numbers on your end."

Ernst Straub came in at five o'clock. "How's he working out?" He addressed Paul without paying attention to Walter.

"He is doing a fine job. Pretty good on his first day."

"All right, then." He went out.

That's it? Could have asked me directly, thought Walter. As if I wasn't even here.

That night, Walter was haunted by numbers—no nightmare, just numbers swirling around in his head. Six-digit numbers, starting with nines, with fours, with fives. Numbers in columns, in rows, disappearing, reappearing. Twos and sevens and zeros. Paul saying numbers, in English, in German. Frank asking for numbers, Straub asking for a number, Roswita giving him a number. Roswita... What's her number?

The alarm clock he had bought in the souvenir shop on the *Berlin* rattled. He awoke in confusion, did not feel rested. Nuts and bolts and springs and washers—all just numbers.

The following Saturday, Walter ventured out to New Jersey— a whole different state. Gerda had given him directions. To save his precious tokens, he set out early and walked the forty blocks along Broadway to the bus terminal. There had been a pre-dawn thunderstorm; the cooling effect evaporated quickly, replaced by the humidity rising from the pavement. It would again be a scorching August day.

He was relieved that the ticket for the Red & Tan bus to New Brunswick was less than three dollars. He bought a bunch of flowers; they looked like the carnations he had once taken to the Pinkerts for Christmas.

Emerging from the Lincoln Tunnel on the other side of the Hudson, Walter had the impression of being in another country, not just another state. No skyscrapers here, but what a view! All of Manhattan, like a city built of Lego blocks, appeared through the windows as the bus climbed to the elevated highway. He recognized the Chrysler and the Empire State buildings. Not even on his arrival in the *Berlin* two weeks earlier had he been able to appreciate the marvel that was Manhattan.

Gerda and Joe met him at the bus station in New Brunswick. Both were in shorts and T-shirt. Walter felt awkward in long pants, dress shirt and jacket.

Gerda greeted him in German. "You had no trouble finding your way?"

"No. You gave me very good directions. It was an interesting bus ride. I brought you these flowers."

She answered with the obligatory, "Ah, you shouldn't have."

"Gerda told me you already speak some English," said Joe. "Today you can practice with us. Because that's what we speak here: English." He balanced on his toes; he was at least two inches shorter than Walter.

Walter had an immediate adverse reaction toward Joe. "Oh, some English... Yes, that's what we speak at work."

On the way to their home in their brand new Chevrolet Bel Air, Gerda explained to her husband that Walter has already been working for one week. "At AID, an automotive company."

They arrived at a tree-lined street with semi-attached houses, each with a front lawn and a driveway that led to the garage. "Here we are," said Gerda. "Different from New York, huh? They call this the Garden State. Our garden is in the back. Come on, I'll show you."

The house was—well, nice. Walter was not overly impressed. Kind of like back home in Rendsburg, but the rooms were larger, loftier and the kitchen more modern than that of his parents.

"We have three bedrooms upstairs, and one and a half baths." Walter thought, what's half a bath? "Come, I'll show you the patio and our pool," said Gerda. They walked through the living room and out through a sliding glass door. "This corner we call our garden." There were a rose bush, some other flowers and a tomato plant, a table with chairs under an umbrella.

Joe came out with tall glasses on a tray. "Pink lemonade. Sit down, tell us about your first impressions of New York. Takes time to adjust. First off, out here we don't wear a suit on the weekend. At work, what do you wear?" He looked over to Gerda. "Automotive, you said? As a mechanic?"

"I am not a mechanic," Walter interrupted Joe. "It's inventory control."

"Oh, so you don't get your hands dirty."

Walter took a sip of the iced lemonade. This conversation, Joe's tone, was not to his liking. "No, I don't get my hands dirty," he said lightly, with a smile.

"Soon you won't miss the furs," Gerda reminded him. "It's not like in Europe."

"You were lucky. Most immigrants don't have it so easy," said Joe. "My parents started out working in the kitchens of Chinese restaurants in San Francisco." Then he talked about himself. "I went to university, have a degree in chemistry and biology. Run the research department at Bristol-Myers. We will soon move to a more affluent neighborhood. We have to. Belong to the Golf and Country Club. Upper crust, you know."

Walter was now at the point where he didn't like Joe at all. "Can I use the bathroom, Gerda?"

"May I," Joe corrected him. "May I use the bathroom. It's important to speak proper English—if you want to move up. Socially, you know."

"Joe, he arrived just two weeks ago. I didn't speak any better at first."

"You had me as a mentor."

She ignored his remark. "Upstairs. You'll find it," Gerda told Walter.

Before he returned to the patio, Walter took off his jacket and draped it over a chair in the living room.

"That's better," Joe exclaimed. "Short sleeves. Sit down. So, what brought you to the United States?"

"Well, a number of things. I was doing all right in Frankfurt in the fur business until my boss brought his son into the firm." He looked over at Gerda. "You remember Hans Pinkert. Did you know his son, Klaus?"

"No. That must have been after I left. Everyone knew Pinkert had something going on in London. Didn't he get divorced?"

"Yes, and then suddenly his son, this eighteen-year old kid, was my boss. Knew nothing about the business, couldn't tell a mink from a raccoon. We called him the snotnose, that arrogant bastard—excuse me. Nobody could stand him. So, we taught him a lesson, my friends and I. His father showed up from London, saw what was going on and closed his business in Frankfurt."

"And you lost your job? You should have handled that situation with his son more intelligently. You see, in circumstances like that…"

"Joe, let Walter tell the story," Gerda admonished her husband.

"He acted foolishly," he answered his wife, then turned back to Walter. "You don't teach your boss a lesson; you find a way to…"

"Anyway, that's how I ended up in Vienna with Leo Reichenberg." Walter saw no reason to make the story any longer.

"And you got yourself into trouble there, too?" Joe hammered away. "Now you want to try your luck here. Let me give you some sound advice. Here things are…"

Walter looked at his watch. He did not come here to be lectured by this self-important, pompous ass. He paid no further attention to what Joe went on and on about, occasionally nodding or shaking his head, pretending he was still listening. Gerda tried her best to direct the conversation elsewhere, but she was only marginally successful.

She served lunch, a green salad with hard-boiled eggs, and Italian bread. Joe continued with explanation about the different customs and habits in the United States.

"In Germany you have your main meal at lunch time, right? Here, a sandwich or a salad, perhaps a hamburger. In the evening it's dinner."

"Joe, I am sure Walter has already…"

"Gerda, I am trying to make it easier for him," and back to Walter, "So, Walter, listen. Let me give you a few hints how to go about…"

A few times Walter tried to bring the conversation around to subjects more familiar to him: his life in the small town where he grew up; his sailing around the islands of Denmark; his time in Frankfurt and Vienna. But each time Joe found a way to correct him, disprove him or dispute what he said.

Walter endured that day with all the patience and restraint he was capable of. Gerda certainly noticed how her husband had made him uncomfortable and that day in August remained his only visit to the Changs in New Brunswick.

Chapter Nine

Walter was well into his second month at AID and the routine of sliding trays with the inventory cards in and out of the slots, looking up numbers and making the appropriate notations had become second nature to him.

"Where are the request forms, Paul? Straub is driving me crazy." Roswita had asked Paul twice before. "He will kill both of us if he doesn't get those requests today." She looked over at Walter. "I think he might spare you." Her laugh was intoxicating.

"Give me an hour. He'll have them before lunch." Paul didn't look up.

Much as Walter tried to meet Roswita alone, it had not happened. The pace of their work was relentless and there never was a slack moment. Could he walk into her office at lunchtime and ask her, in the presence of Mister Straub, to have lunch with him? Would that be grounds for dismissal? He was still under probation. Could he ask her to have a coke with him at the afternoon break? What would Paul's reaction be?

She certainly had a sense of humor. How could she bear working in that cubicle, face to face with strict and humorless Mister Straub?

Roswita came into the inventory room. "Guten Morgen, Ihr zwee beeden," she said in the broadest of Saxon dialect. "The two of you." She plunked a stack of papers on the desk in the corner. "Straub said these have to go out today. How are you doing, Walter?" She lightly put a hand on his shoulder. It felt like an electric shock to him.

"Roswita, I wanted to ask..." he began. She was already out the door, back to her cubicle. Damn, there's just no way. Is she coy? Hard to get, or what?

Walter explored alternative lunch places at Queensboro Plaza and decided on a pizza parlor he had visited before. A stool at the counter became available and he ordered a couple of slices with mushrooms and pepperoni.

"Walter," he heard his name in a familiar voice. Roswita Peschel sat at a table with two girls from the office. "There's a chair for you here."

My lucky day has come, Walter whispered to himself. With his two slices of pizza on a paper plate and a coke in hand, he joined the girls at their table.

"Fernanda and Grace," Roswita introduced her companions. "This is Walter."

"I was wondering when I would run into you," he said to the threesome, but he meant only Roswita. Neither Fernanda nor Grace was of any interest to him.

Grace stood up. "Come on. Finished with that pizza? I want to show you the dress I'm going to buy."

"Nice meeting you," said Fernanda or Grace.

"Sorry, Walter. See you later," Roswita called back as they hurried out the door.

Girls. Looking at a dress... Sorry, Walter. See you later. What does that mean? Walter finished his pizza, took a sip of his coke and left. He lingered for a moment on the street. There was a dress shop. Is that where they went? Oh, what the hell. He went back to work.

On his way home in the evening in the crowded train, sweaty and squeezed in among other sweaty bodies, Walter was looking forward to a shower and changing into fresh clothes before going to Nathan's or White Castle. Two hot dogs and a large iced tea for under two dollars was all his budget permitted.

Mrs. Nieves met him at the door. "Mister Hansen, do you like meatloaf? Miss Ponce is having dinner with me tonight. You can come, too, if you don't have other plans."

"Thank you, very kind of you. I would like that, if it's no inconvenience."

"Let's say at seven? I also have a bottle of beer for you, left by Mister McGee. He moved out last week, you know."

"Mister McGee? Frank? No, I didn't know that."

Nilda Ponce came in and greeted Julia Nieves in Spanish. Walter received no more than a nod.

"Seven o'clock all right, Nilda? Mister Hansen will be having dinner with us."

"Está bien, Señora. Gracias." She went to her room.

Walter had not yet figured her out. She was quite good looking, in an exotic way, with her short black hair, Latin features and olive skin tone.

Actually, Nilda was the type Walter usually found attractive, but again his thoughts turned to Roswita. Why am I so intrigued by her? Must be her outgoing nature, and then so... so, what's the word? Coy? Bashful? Maybe playful. Anyway, intriguing.

111

In his room, Walter found two letters. One was from his mother, the other from Ilse. Shortly after his arrival in New York, he had sent a postcard to his friends in Frankfurt, telling them that he had walked away from the fur business. He resisted the urge to open Ilse's letter, not to be late for dinner at Mrs. Nieves's table, and just quickly glanced through the lines his mother wrote, then showered and dressed in sport shirt and slacks.

Nilda had changed from her white medical outfit into a light colored summer dress. Julia Nieves turned on the big electric fan in the dining room. "Meatloaf, mashed potatoes and asparagus," she announced. "Please, help yourselves. Your beer, Mister Hansen. It's Heineken."

"Thank you, Mrs. Nieves. May I ask you to call me Walter? It would really please me. I hear you call Miss Ponce by her first name."

"All right. Walter it is."

"And I am Nilda. May I call you Walter, too?"

"Of course—eh, Nilda." Did she actually address me directly? To avoid an awkward moment, he added, "You are from Puerto Rico. I hear it is quite beautiful. I hope to have the opportunity some day to visit your island."

Mrs. Nieves said, "Walter is from Germany."

"Yes, I know. You told me."

They ate the meatloaf and the mashed potatoes and the asparagus. "This is very good, Mrs. Nieves," said Walter to break the silence. "Thanks for inviting me." He poured some Heineken into his glass.

"I am glad you like it."

Walter touched the napkin to his lips. "Mrs. Nieves, do you have a new boarder to take Mister McGee's room? Not that I don't like my room; it's comfortable, but to the back. My window faces the wall of the adjacent building."

Nilda said something in Spanish to which Mrs. Nieves replied with a nod.

"Mister... I am sorry, Walter. Nilda has someone who might like the room. I will let you know tomorrow."

"Oh, of course."

"By the way, did you find the two letters that came for you today? I put them on the dresser in your room."

"Yes, Mrs. Nieves. Thank you. I will read them later." As far as he could tell from briefly scanning his mother's short letter, there was nothing of interest. Now, Ilse... that was a different matter.

After sitting through nearly an hour of small talk at the dinner table, Walter at last returned to his room and eagerly opened Ilse's envelope. He was not surprised, but disappointed, to find only half a page in her pointed handwriting.

Walter, how are you? Not much has changed here, except Jürgen is now in London with Interfurs and I am again with Pudding. He sends regards. I haven't seen the others much. Leo Reichenberg was in town last week. Jürgen saw Pinkert and his snotnose son in London. How's New York? I try to imagine you among all those skyscrapers. Write to me, if you want. My new address is on the envelope. Kisses, Ilse.

Reading she was back with Pudding gave Walter a momentary sting. The rest was of no consequence. He had distanced himself. However, Ilse had been his first real encounter with the opposite sex. He decided to write to her, but not just yet. There was Roswita, and now even Nilda crammed into his head. He picked up his mother's letter, read again *to be careful, to eat right, not to trust strangers*. Then that one sentence about his father who could not understand that his son abandoned the fur trade. *...for generations in our families*. How can I make him understand? he thought. He will never understand.

A knock at his door brought him out of his reverie. "Yes, what is it? Come in, please." He went to open the door.

There stood Nilda. "Mrs. Nieves asks if you perhaps wanted to watch a movie with us on the TV in her living room. It's Charlie Chaplin."

What's going on here? Nilda, Charlie Chaplin, Roswita, Ilse... What the hell is going on? "Charlie Chaplin? Is he...? Isn't he...?" He was too surprised to think quickly. "I was, ah, I was going to write a letter. But, of course, that can wait. Sure. In Mrs. Nieves's living room?"

"Yes. That's where the TV is. But, if you have something else... I just ask, I mean Mrs. Nieves asked."

"Okay, thank you. Tell Mrs. Nieves I would be happy to watch the movie with her and you."

"It starts at eight, in a few minutes."

Chapter Ten

Three months to the day after Walter began his employment at AID, the Personnel manager called him to his office. "As of today you will be enrolled in the company insurance plan. You'll receive a raise of five dollars, but a portion of that goes toward your premium. There will be little difference in your paycheck. Okay? That's it. Back to work."

"Thank you, sir." Walter had expected a review, or at least some sort of evaluation, at the end of his probation period, but at AID, time was too costly for lengthy discussions and deliberations. He went back to the inventory control room.

Paul looked up. "Everything okay?"

"I guess so. I am enrolled in the insurance plan, he told me. Does that mean I am in? Oh, and I'll get a raise, but that goes toward the insurance, he said."

"Yeah, you're in. Hand me those orders, will you? We're a little behind."

That day, Walter remembered, was exactly four weeks after that dinner invitation, the meatloaf dinner, followed by a Charlie Chaplin movie. Ten minutes into the film, Mrs. Nieves was fast asleep and Nilda, sitting next to him on the couch, suddenly, without any preamble, turned and kissed him wildly on the mouth. At the same time Walter was aware of her hand on his crotch. Then Nilda had quickly left the room without a word. Charlie Chaplin waddled, cane in hand, across the TV screen.

Walter did not know what to do. He decided he couldn't just leave his hostess, so he stayed, absentmindedly watching the movie. He could not understand then, and even four weeks later had no full understanding of this neurotic, psychotic or somehow disturbed young woman.

When Mrs. Nieves awoke that evening, some time before the end of the movie, Walter excused himself, saying that he perhaps had overstayed and that Miss Nilda had already retired. He then knocked at Nilda's door. She let him in, but immediately backed away as he came toward her.

"No, no. Please. It's not right. You must go." She covered her face with her hands. "You must go, you must go, please. I am… It's not right. I am not…"

"Nilda, it's okay. There is no reason to… Please, believe me, it is okay."

She then began to cry hysterically. "I made a mistake, I am sorry. It was not right. I was confused, I thought… Please leave now. It was a mistake." She sobbed, "I will never be able to, to, to…"

"Nilda. Please, believe me. Nothing happened. Don't cry. You did nothing wrong. I'll go now. See you tomorrow."

"No, no."

"What? Don't go? Or what?"

"No, go."

That was four weeks ago. He did not see her the next morning, nor in the evening, and he did not ask Mrs. Nieves if she had seen her. It was not until several days after the incident that they met on the street in front of their building. Nilda was taciturn, nodded and did not meet his glance. Just like before, thought Walter. Perhaps better this way, but what caused her to act the way she did that evening and then regret it so violently? He felt sympathy, perhaps something like pity for her. And yet, she had aroused a desire in him. There had been so much passion in her kiss, in her touch.

The day Walter's position at AID was confirmed, he was in good spirits. As he left the office, Roswita waved to him and blew him a kiss. "One of these days..." he hummed to himself. In the diner at Queensboro Plaza he had a steak sandwich and a bottle of Miller's to celebrate the day. Before going home, he had another beer at the corner of 79th and Broadway.

The room that Frank McGee had vacated and that Nilda's cousin had occupied for a couple of weeks, was again empty. Walter knocked at Mrs. Nieves's door.

"Mrs. Nieves, not that it matters much, but what about that room? I would really like it. Or is Miss Ponce's cousin coming back?"

"No, I don't think so. Why don't you ask her when she comes in."

"Yes, thank you. I will."

Nilda arrived shortly after that and Walter met her in the hall. "Nilda, excuse me, may I ask about your cousin? Is she coming back? If not, I would like that room."

"My cousin? Oh yes, Elena. I don't think she's coming back. But—that room, it's right next to mine. I would rather, I mean, I don't think it would be right." She opened her door. "Good night."

Walter had the vague beginnings of understanding something, not sure yet, of course, but an uncertain inkling stirred in his mind. Her cousin? Maybe not. "Nilda, may I talk to you?"

She hesitated, halfway in the door, but did not turn to face him. "What is it?"

"May I come in? It has nothing to do with, you know, that night when we watched Charlie Chaplin. Well, yes, it has something to do with it. All I want to know: are you all right? I mean, you can talk to me."

She sat on her bed. Walter followed her into the room and closed the door. He stood in front of her, looking down on her shiny black hair.

She did not look up at him. "What is it you want to know?" She whispered.

Walter felt intensely close to her at that moment, something like love for this fragile, tangled woman. So small, he thought, so helpless. He sat next to her, took her in his arms and she let him. Her tears soaked his shirt as he slowly, softly held her against his chest.

They made love that night. First, very gently, he kissed her, the way a woman might kiss woman and she responded. When he moved his face next to hers, she averted her eyes but did not resist his love making as a man to a woman.

They lay togethr in silence. After a long time, Walter, in a soft voice, said her name. He repeated, "Nilda, it is all right, isn't it?"

She stirred. "I want to be alone now." As if speaking in a dream, she added, "You understand me. You understand me now. I am not who I am. You know who I am. I want to know who I am. Please, go now. I want to know who I am." Her voice drifted off.

"You are Nilda. I know who you are." He spoke soothingly, with infinite care. Quietly he left her room.

Toward the end of the month, winter arrived in New York. The first snow flurries twirled on Macy's Thanksgiving parade. Walter and Nilda stood among the crowd on the sidewalk on Central Park West.

"You did not go to Puerto Rico for the holiday. Why?"

"I simply didn't go."

"Nilda, why? I know it isn't because of me. Is it because of your cousin?"

"Look! Popeye the Sailorman! Here come the police on horseback. Elena? She's not my cousin. There's Pluto! He looks half deflated."

"Yes. I think I knew that. She is your lover. Don't you still love her?"

"I betrayed her. With you. Let's not wait for Santa Claus. I don't like him." She held on to his arm as they stepped back from the curb amid the cheering crowd. "I don't know my way from here. I betrayed her long before the other night. In my mind. With you. I didn't tell her, but she knew."

"I had no idea. You never even looked at me." Walter led her across the street through the gap between a marching band and baton-twirling cheerleaders. They walked along Eighty-first Street, away from the music and the applause. "But do you love her? Does she still love you?"

"Who? Elena? I don't want her to love me. And I don't want to love her. I don't want you to love me either and I know you don't." Her tone became harsh. "You have pity on me. I don't want your pity. I don't want anybody, anything." She let go of his arm. "I don't know what I want."

Silently they walked to the end of the block. Walter swallowed before he spoke in a soft voice. "Ah, I'll see if the drugstore on Broadway is open. Thanks for going to the parade with me."

She nodded and they went their separate ways. A confused, deeply disturbed human being, Walter reflected. In turmoil—at the brink of falling apart. She was right, though: he did not love her. He pitied her, but his pity was genuine; he wished he could help her find her way, not for his sake, but for hers.

Of course, the drugstore was closed; it was Thanksgiving. Walter walked along the almost deserted Broadway. At Sixty-eighth Street he found an Irish Pub that was open. He entered the smoke filled bar. A few characters sat at the counter.

He ordered a whisky, paid for it, but before he drank, a picture crept into his mind. Nilda—what if she…? He took one sip of his drink and left the bar.

Music drifted from Nilda's room, some Latin folk tune. Walter stood outside her door and listened for moment, then went into his room, took off his coat and stretched out on his bed. She must be all right, he thought relieved.

A moment later he jumped up, ran across the hallway and knocked at her door. "Nilda, are you all right? Answer me!"

She opened the door. "What do you mean? Of course I am all right. You want to come in?"

"No, no. That's okay. It's just, I wanted to make sure."

"Make sure, what? You thought I might…" she made a gesture, like cutting her wrist. "Don't be silly," she laughed.

"It's all clear to me now. I know who I am, what I am. So, don't worry. I made up my mind."

"About what?"

"You'll see. I'll go to Puerto Rico for Christmas, to see my family, and perhaps…"

"Elena?"

"Sure. Why not?"

"I am glad."

"Mrs. Nieves went to Long Island. She left me some turkey with rice and cranberry sauce in the refrigerator. We can eat together, if you like. I am sure there is enough for two. Everything is closed today; it is Thanksgiving, you know."

AID did not give their employees the Friday off, as did so many other companies. Half the staff had taken a vacation day. Roswita, too, was absent. Mister Straub, for once, was in a relaxed mood. Only a handful of orders came in. Paul and Walter used the free time to check some of the inventory cards that showed discrepancies.

Walter reflected on the evening before. Nilda had heated the rice, the turkey and the gravy in the kitchen and they ate together at the dining table, just the two of them. It was all so normal. They had a glass of red wine. Nilda told him of San Juan, her parents and her childhood; Walter talked about Germany, Vienna and his sailing adventure. It was all so normal. There was even some laughter, and he did not let the sudden transformation in Nilda trouble him.

At three o'clock, Mister Straub came into the inventory room. "Get everything done? We are closing at four today. See that nothing is left over and then go home."

Walter dreaded the approaching holidays. For the first time he would be alone on Christmas. In Frankfurt he had had his friends. In Vienna, Leo Reichenberg had given him the train fare to visit his parents.

Before going home, he cashed his paycheck at the Chase Manhattan bank and then bought some Christmas cards at the Five-and-Dime store—the cheapest he could find, a box of twelve for a dollar seventy-five. What a waste of money, he thought; plus the stamps.

On the dresser in his room lay a letter from his mother; the mere sight of it pierced his conscience. Six weeks since her last letter, and he had not answered. What could he write? That he had sex with Nilda? That he really wanted Roswita?

There was another envelope, with no return address. He opened it first.

Walter, how are you? Haven't seen or heard from you. Joe and I would like you to come out and spend Christmas Day with us. Give me a call or stop by the office. Gerda.

Yeah right, he chuckled. The only thing worse than being alone on Christmas would be spending the day with Joe Chang. Reluctantly, he opened his mother's letter.

Complaining, disappointed, disillusioned. *How can you be so ungrateful? Your father is embittered and depressed. Our only son... We made all the sacrifices.*

He knew that was coming, and resolved to write—tomorrow, or the day after. That invitation from Gerda Chang he did not even consider seriously. He just had to find an excuse, make up a story.

At lunchtime on Monday, he called her at Bernard Goldsmith's office. "Gerda, so nice of you and Joe to invite me. I would have loved it, but Paul, my supervisor here at AID, asked me to come out to Flushing and spend Christmas Day with him and his wife."

"Oh, well, okay then. We had not heard from you. I thought, you know, maybe you didn't like the way Joe talked to you. He sounded a little patronizing, but he only wanted to help, you know."

"No, no. Nothing like that. I'm just working so hard, my job is very demanding. In the evenings I am dead tired. I would have come by your office, but you know... I can't. No time. Just taking a minute to call and thank you."

"Maybe New Year's Day, then. How's that?"

"Oh." He wasn't prepared for that. "I don't know. I'll let you know." He made believe his boss was calling him and shouted out, "Yes, Mister Straub. Be right there. Sorry, Gerda. I have to go. Say hello to Mister Goldsmith, and, of course, to Joe."

Franz walked by. "Straub? He's in his office."

Walter grinned. "I know."

Christmas approached. Decorations were put up in shop windows; Santas rang bells in front of department stores and garlands stretched from lamppost to lamppost. Walter wrote a few Christmas cards: to Ilse, to Pudding and to Leo Reichenberg who had always been so generous to him. Then he addressed one to Joe and Gerda Chang. I have very few friends, he thought. I wish I had Roswita's address.

He could no longer put off writing to his parents. *Liebe Eltern,* he started. *Sorry I did not write sooner. I was sick.* He ripped the card up. What am I doing? He took a new card from the box. *Liebe Eltern,* he began. *Sorry I did not write sooner.* For a long time he did not know what to say. Then, *I met a girl, her name is Roswita.* He tore that one up, too. On another card he wrote, *Liebe Eltern.* Nothing came to his mind.

He went out. The city was quiet on this cold but sunny Sunday afternoon. He directed his steps along Eighty-first Street toward the Hudson River. A tugboat pulled a string of barges upstream; the Circle Line sightseeing boat carried only a handful of passengers. Few people were about in Riverside Park. He strolled along as far as to the Sailors and Soldiers Monument and then turned into Eighty-sixth Street to have something to eat in one of the German restaurants. The sun was hiding behind the tall buildings on Fifth Avenue and the air became chilly. Walter gave up on the idea of a German café. Instead, he went into Gimbels at the corner of Lexington Avenue. The department store was crowded with shoppers. Walter had no need to buy a gift for anyone. He took a seat at the lunch counter and ordered a ham-and-cheese sandwich.

He had hoped that a walk would clear his mind enough to come up with a few lines to write to his parents, but when he arrived back home, he still had nothing.

The wall of the adjacent building was so close to his window, even in the day time his room remained semi-dark. At five o'clock, Walter turned on the light and, as he flicked the switch, simultaneously a bulb lit up in his head. He sat down quickly, not to lose his thought, and wrote on the card he had started earlier to his parents, *it has been six weeks that I last heard from you. I hope you are both well. I am fine, work is demanding and leaving no time to think, the days and weeks fly by almost unnoticed. I hope to hear from you soon. And,* he almost forgot, *Merry Christmas! Your son Walter.* He read it over. Yes, that's good. It gets right back at them. Loving concern, and avoiding his mother's accusation of being ungrateful. All in a few lines. Brilliant!

The week started with a heavy workload. "It's always like this before Christmas," said Paul. "It's like people give car parts as Christmas gifts."

They worked feverishly until noon break. Walter had brought some leftover turkey for lunch and joined Paul and Franz in the lager. They cleared a table and sat down together.

"Mister Straub asked me to come over to his house for Christmas," said Franz. "He's a friend of my family back home in Stuttgart, you know."

"Is he married?" asked Walter.

"No. His wife died years ago. He lives alone, but has plenty of friends. He is very different in private."

Paul said, "But on Christmas Day my wife and I always hold a kind of open house. Aren't you coming over, then? You, too, Walter."

"Oh, I am sure we will be dropping in. Thanks, Paul."

"Yeah, thanks, Paul," Walter added.

Straub came into the lager. "Come on, wrap it up. Back to work. Orders are coming in like a blizzard."

It all came together for Walter. He would not be alone on Christmas and he hasn't been lying to Gerda, after all.

The Friday before Christmas was not a payday, but Roswita came in and handed both Paul and Walter an envelope. "Bonus time!" she called out cheerfully, then went into the lager with the envelopes for the workers there.

Walter opened his. "Thirty dollars. What did you get?" he asked Paul.

"One week's salary. You are here less than half a year." He did not interrupt his work. "You're coming on Christmas Day? Take the Flushing train to the last stop, then the bus on Main Street. Get off at the third stop. It's right there."

"Thanks," said Walter. "In the afternoon, right?"

Roswita returned from the lager on her way back to her office. "See you, Paul. Merry Christmas, Walter." She was gone before Walter could say anything.

"Yes, in the afternoon. She'll be there, too. Usually comes with one or both of her roommates."

"Fernanda and...?"

"No, she lives with two stewardesses. In Jackson Heights, I think."

Walter wasn't sure what to bring to an open house party. He knew that Paul was married. In Germany it would be flowers. Again he was reminded of that Christmas Day at the Pinkerts, years ago.

From Mrs. Nieves he learned that Nilda had left that morning for Puerto Rico. "She will not be back until after New Years." He was disappointed that she had not told him, but lately they had not seen each other. It could be that she was avoiding him again, but, he thought, that's okay.

"What would be appropriate to bring to a party, Mrs. Nieves? A Christmas party. An open house, they called it."

"Open house? Actually, I don't think you have to bring anything; but, if you want to, a bottle of wine is always appreciated. Give it to the lady of the house, if there is one."

"Thank you. Was Miss Ponce all right? I have not seen her around."

126

"Oh, she was fine. I saw her much happier lately. I wonder if she might have found a nice young man. I would be happy for her."

Nilda. She had it all figured out, she told Walter. She knew who she was, she said. He was not quite sure what that meant. Probably that she would reconcile with Elena, but would that mean that Elena would be coming back with her? That would be all right with him, except he would never get the room he still wanted. When he asked Mrs. Nieves again for it, she answered, "Let's wait until the New Year, when Nilda comes back." Evidently, Mrs. Nieves had no clue.

That year, Christmas Day fell on a Monday. Walter had spent Christmas Eve like any other Sunday, except that he shopped for a bottle of wine. He remembered the wild poker evenings in Frankfurt with his friends, and the cheap wine they used to drink. Oh, what fun that was! Rolf and Jürgen would get drunk, and then they joked about Ilse's taste buds they all had tasted. "Just don't fall in love with her," they told him. "She's not the type to fall in love with." Walter fell in love with her anyway, or… he liked her an awful lot. He still did.

This is not the time to reminisce, he told himself. Tomorrow I will at last have a chance to get to know Roswita Peschel, what she is like, how it would be to… There was a knock at his door.

"Yes, Mrs. Nieves." He opened the door. "Come in, please."

"Walter, it's Christmas Eve. I don't want to disturb you, but I have a little something for you." She handed him a small package. "It's nothing, really, but I thought you might like it."

He took the package from her. "It's heavy," he said. "I am sorry, I have nothing…" He was embarrassed. I should have thought of that.

"No, no," she said. "You don't have to. Good night." She went out and closed the door.

Walter unwrapped the package. It was his first acquaintance with the Christmas cake he had heard about, the one nobody ever ate and always passed on to someone else. He looked at it and saw only glazed fruit and nuts, glued together with brown, sticky molasses. To him it did not have the semblance of cake at all, with that waxy paper baked into it all around the sides. What am I supposed to do with it? Certainly not eat it. Who knows through how many hands this wonder of Christmas has already gone. Maybe it will keep until next year. He put it back in the box. "Enough with the cake already," he said out loud, then looked at the door to make sure it was closed. There were other, more pressing and more interesting things to mull over.

Chapter Eleven

Walter arrived at Paul's house between three and four in the afternoon on Christmas Day. Paul introduced him to his wife, Elisabeth, and to a couple with a small child, their neighbors. A punch bowl was on the table and the Christmas tree was lit.

"Mrs. Kempowski, I brought you a bottle of wine." Walter unwrapped the Beaujolais and handed it to her. "I hope you like it."

"Danke, that is nice. Let me have your coat. Please, sit down. Have a glass of punch," she said in heavy accented English. They resumed their conversation and Walter found it difficult to join in. He sipped from his glass. A little sweet, but not bad.

When the baby started crying and the neighbors had to tend to it, Paul said to Walter, "People will be coming and going all through the afternoon. They start coming in late and the last of them leave by nine or ten."

"I guess I came too early, then. May I have another glass of punch? It's very good." He hoped to get the strawberry that stuck to the bottom to float.

"Help yourself. Nonsense. Stay as long as you like. Later some from the office will show up."

Walter ladled punch into his glass and swirled it. The strawberry popped up. "People from the office? Roswita and some of her friends, you mean? Franz said he might show up with Straub."

"You like Roswita? She's a wildcat, I tell you. Flirts with everybody. I put her in her place early on. I didn't need that. Six months after I came from Germany I sent for Elisabeth and we got married."

"Really? I mean... So, you got married here." Elisabeth was homely, quite the opposite of Roswita. "You have a nice home, Paul." He could not leave the remark about Roswita without a response. "Roswita... Is she really like that? You think she sleeps around, huh?"

"I didn't say that. I said she flirts with everybody. Whatever else she does, I don't know."

That was as far as Walter wanted to take it, and the doorbell ended the subject. Elisabeth answered the door. More people Walter did not know entered the living room. Cookies and Christmas Stollen were passed around and they all had a glass of punch; the bowl seemed bottomless, but then the glasses weren't too big. Walter joined in the trivial conversation with whatever seemed to fit. He resisted looking at his watch. Some of the guests left, while others came. So this is an open house, he thought. What if she is not coming? The doorbell again, and Walter sneaked a look at his watch. Five thirty. He heard the booming voice of Ernst Straub. There weren't enough chairs for all the people that now filled the room. Walter stood up and grasped Mister Straub's outstretched hand. Franz came forward from behind Straub. They shook hands. The conversation became more animated and Walter felt less awkward as they stood in smaller groups.

Roswita, tall and thin with a tousled mane of blond hair, arrived shortly after seven. "Hi Paul. Elisabeth, how are you? Oh, Mister Straub, Merry Christmas!" She opened her trench coat, but kept it on. The hem of her coat met the top of her boots below the knees. A glass of punch in her hand, she acknowledged Walter and Franz who stood at the opposite side of the table. "Hello, Ihr zwee beeden!" she greeted them in her strong Saxon dialect across the crowd that had accumulated.

A stunning brunette, only a little shorter than Roswita, had come in with her. Walter worked his way around the table.

"Walter, this is Felicia Napolitano. Felix, I told you about Walter, remember?"

"Hello," said Walter, and to Roswita, "You talk to people behind my back?"

Roswita laughed, "Only good things."

"Good things? What do you know about me?" To Felix he said, "She doesn't know anything about me."

Franz came over to them. "Hi, Roswita. Who's your good-looking friend?"

"Oh, Franz, behave yourself."

"I am Felicia," said Felix in a dusky voice that matched her tanned complexion. She wore a baseball cap over her shoulder-length brown hair, a short beige coat and boots.

Walter was surprised by Franz's outgoing approach. "Yeah, behave yourself, Franz," he joked.

"Paul, you met Felicia Napolitano, right?"

"I don't think so. May I take your coats?"

"We're not staying long, Paul. Just came in to say Merry Christmas."

"Okay," he said and turned away. A little abrupt, thought Walter. Doesn't he see these are two gorgeous girls?

"So, where are you headed?" asked Franz.

131

"None of your business," Roswita laughed, but Felix said, "Friends."

Walter did not want his chances to slip away. "I was just about to leave when you came. Maybe one more glass of punch? Then I'll walk out with you."

"Friends? Another party?" Franz asked. "Can we go, too?"

Now he is downright pushy, thought Walter. "Franz, you just got here with Herr Straub. Don't you think you should…"

"That doesn't mean I have to stick with him."

"They can both come, right, Roxy?" That smoky voice was doing something to Walter.

Roxy? Felix? He was getting suspicious. Oh Jesus, I hope not, he thought. Let Franz have Felix, although I don't think he'd have a chance with her. She is way out of his league and she doesn't seem to care for either one of us.

They climbed into Felicia's yellow and black Beetle, Franz and Walter in the backseat.

"Felix, put the top down. I need fresh air after that stuffiness," Roswita exploded. "Boy, they were stuffy! How much time did we waste there? Oh no, that's not right. They are nice people. So nice. Too nice. It's all too nice. Now let's have some fun. Wait a minute, where are you going, Felix?"

"Roll down the window and control yourself. And control that accent of yours."

"I controlled myself. Wasn't I gracious? And my accent? That's my personality. That's who I am." She rolled down the window and turned to face Walter and Franz in the back. "Wasn't I gracious, guys?"

Franz said, "You were gracious, except to me. 'Behave yourself', what was that all about, huh?"

"You were funny," said Walter. "And your accent, I like it."

"Thank you, Walter. You see? That's being gracious." Her carefully disarrayed white-blond hair tangled in the cold breeze that came through the window. She turned back to Felix. "Where are we going? We're going back to our place, right?"

Felicia knew her way around. She was a born New Yorker. There was no snow on the streets and she drove fast, swept along with the traffic on Queens Boulevard. In Elmhurst, she turned into a tree-lined side street and stopped a few houses down.

"Stay in the car. I'll just be a second. I promised her."

Franz asked, "No party?"

"What the hell," escaped Roswita as Felix crossed the sidewalk and rang the bell at the single-family home. She shifted in her seat and leaned back toward Walter. "What do you know?"

Walter shrugged. "About what?"

"Friends of her's." She whispered, "You know, she is... She is—you know."

"And you?" Walter asked carefully. She gave him a very quick, very sharp look. "I mean, I'm glad you're not," he affirmed.

Franz had no clue. He was mesmerized by Felicia.

Later that evening they arrived at Jackson Heights. Meg, the girl Felix brought back with them from the house at the tree-lined street in Elmhurst, had been sardined into the backseat of the VW with Walter and Franz. Roswita had met her once before at their doorstep. "This is Megan," Felicia had introduced her briefly. "We were just leaving."

The two-bedroom apartment Roswita Peschel and Felicia Napolitano shared with a third young woman was near Astoria Boulevard. Planes taking off or landing at nearby La Guardia passed so low over the houses they seemed to scrape the rooftops with their landing gears. "Claire's not home," Felicia said to Roswita over the roar of a plane soaring overhead. "She's in Toronto or Montreal." Both Felicia and Claire were stewardesses with TWA.

Franz and Walter stood in the living room, looking at the walls, the sofa, the table, the chairs and at each other. Megan was not much to look at in her shapeless sweater, ill-fitting jeans and mousy-brown hair.

Felix hung up their coats in the hall while Roswita took a bottle of Four Roses from a cabinet and soda water from the refrigerator. Meg, quite familiar with everything around the house, knew where to find the glasses.

"Let me do that." Walter took the bottle from Roswita. "You have ice cubes?"

"Meg, get the ice," said Felicia.

"Felix," Roswita summoned her. "May I talk to you?" She maneuvered her into the first bedroom. "What the hell are you doing? There's three of us living here: Claire, you and I. Not Megan, or whatever her name is. I thought you and Claire… I am all right with that. But now, behind my back… Does Claire know about this Megan?"

"I guess. We're not exclusive. I don't know what she does when I am away in Amsterdam or Zurich."

"Does she sleep here, and I have never noticed?"

134

"You bring guys into the house I don't know."

"Yeah, but they don't live here."

A plane thundered overhead, made the windows rattle. Felix waited until the noise dwindled. "You want to sleep with Walter? Go ahead. I don't tell you what to do."

"What about Franz?"

"I don't sleep with guys."

"I don't mean that. Walter tried to leave him at Paul's party. Why did you say it was okay to bring him along?"

"I tried to be gracious, like you. Anyway, it's your problem now. Let's go back in there and have a drink."

Walter had poured whisky over the ice cubes in their glasses; Meg added some soda to her's. She sat on the sofa, Walter and Franz uncomfortably on the chairs they had pulled away from the dining table. Franz asked her, "Are you, too, flying the friendly skies?"

"No."

"What do you do?" Walter followed up.

"School. NYU."

"She studies foreign affairs," Felicia explained as she and Roswita rejoined the others. Franz handed them their drinks.

"Domestic, too," Roswita added, laughing hilariously. "Especially domestic, ha ha. Merry Christmas!" She took a long swig from her glass.

"Roxy, why do you do that?"

"Oh, come on, Felix. Let's have some fun." She went to put a record on the turntable. Frank Sinatra crooned *What is this Thing called Love.* "Walter and Franz have to be at work tomorrow morning. I plan to take the day off. Mister Straub will not be pleasant. About Franz leaving him at Paul's place, I mean."

"He might be hung over," Franz suggested.

"He's never hung over. Not with that weak punch they had there."

Felicia and Megan danced, slow and tight. Franz's jaw dropped. He looked at Walter who mouthed silently, "Now you get it?"

"Want to dance, Franz?" Roswita asked him. "Come on. Like those two lovebirds." She already had him by the sleeve.

"Ah, I don't know," he said uncertainly, getting up from his chair. "You're not, you know?"

"Hell no. Walter can tell you that."

"Me? How can I tell?"

"You will, before the night is over."

"Ah, I better get going," Franz stumbled. "Work tomorrow, it's past midnight

Chapter Twelve

On Tuesday morning, the day after Christmas, Walter felt uncomfortable going to work in the same clothes he had worn the day before, except for the tie Roswita had given him. "Put this on," she told him. "It's one of Felicia's. She sometimes dresses rather manly." It was yellow, with bluish paisley, and did not clash too badly with his gray suit. Neither Paul nor Mister Straub seemed to pay any attention.

"Morning, Paul," he said as he came into the inventory room a couple of minutes before nine. "Nice party yesterday."

"You left early with Franz and Roswita and that other girl, eh, young lady. We kept going till ten o'clock. Even Straub stayed for at least an hour. Did you go some place else?"

"Yeah, their friends, you know. No big deal. I went home right after Franz left."

"We won't have much work today, but tomorrow we start with the inventory. We usually work overtime until New Year's, maybe even on Saturday."

Franz came in from the lager, "Hey, Paul. Nice party." Then, with a sheepish smile he turned to Walter. "That was something, man. I got out of there…"

"Yes, it was," Walter cut him off. "I left right after you. As you said, it was late. And then work today, so…"

"Ah, I get it." He raised an eyebrow as if to say: same suit, borrowed tie. "Talk to you later." He gave Walter a thumbs-up. Paul's back was turned.

Ernst Straub came in. "All right, you are here. You can start with the inventory today. Is Franz in? There won't be many orders. Roswita took a vacation day." He went into the lager.

At noontime, they stopped all outgoing shipments and began the tedious job of counting every item in storage, from nuts and bolts, washers and springs, some as small as a grain of rice, to engine blocks and transmissions. The results were noted on lists imprinted with the item numbers and descriptions.

As the lists came in from the lager, Paul and Walter checked them against the inventory cards. That first afternoon they found few discrepancies. "Use the red marker to highlight the number and put our count in this column. Those we get back to later," said Paul. "They have to recount them out there and we have to check our additions and subtractions." By the end of the day they had uncovered half a dozen errors, but they had thousands of items to go.

On his way home in the evening, he wondered if Mrs. Nieves had noticed that he had not been home over night. Of course, she noticed. I wasn't there for breakfast. He was not concerned about that. I don't have to have an excuse. She's not my mother.

"I had two soft boiled eggs for you in the morning, Walter, and your toast," Mrs. Nieves greeted him in the hall. "Then it came to me that I had not heard you coming in last night. I had company. I hope you had a good time, your first Christmas away from home."

"Yes, Mrs. Nieves. Thank you. It had become quite late and so I stayed over at a friend's house." That sounded like an excuse. I didn't have to say that. "Sorry, next time I'll let you know in advance. Because of breakfast, I mean."

The following three days they did not leave the office before ten at night. On Friday, in an effort to finish counting and recounting, they worked until midnight. Walter took some of the cards that still showed discrepancies home with him. Clamps and fuel line fittings for Porsche and VW were off and had to be reconciled. Adding and subtracting, correcting errors, looking at the small numbers on the cards made his eyes burn and his mind shut down by three in the morning.

Awake at seven, he showered and, without breakfast, took the subway to Queens, a much longer trip on a Saturday morning. Paul and Walter, Franz and some of the warehouse workers corrected a few more mistakes and when Ernst Straub came before lunch, he authorized the remaining items to be adjusted so that the New Year would start without discrepancies between the physical count and the inventory cards.

The diner at the corner opposite the AID building was closed. "Let's go to the hamburger place down the street," said Paul.

Walter took Franz aside. "Look, Paul doesn't have to know what happened the other day, you know, Christmas. Keep your mouth shut on that, okay?"

"Sure. I don't know what happened. You mean, something happened?"

During the week between Christmas and the New Year, there had been hardly any opportunities for Walter and Roswita to talk, or even exchange a glance. She was busy in her cubicle adding the dollar amounts to the inventory figures and transferring the completed lists to the accounting department. Straub did not allow overtime for her, and the one time Walter met her at the soda machine in the lager, she said, "Hi Walter, having fun checking all your rods and nuts? They're important, you know." She laughed, poked him lightly in the chest with her soda can and hurried back to her office. Rods and nuts... Walter shook his head. She's crazy. What about New Year's, he wanted to ask, but she gave him no chance.

Then, on Friday, when she came into the inventory room to pick up completed lists, she left him a piece of paper with a number on it. Just a number.

Nilda Ponce returned to New York with Elena, which meant he could not switch to the front room, but now he was no longer interested. Elena was younger than Nilda, more his age, he guessed. He had not paid much attention to her when for two weeks she occupied the room Frank McGee had vacated. That was before the evening of meatloaf and Charlie Chaplin, and that bizarre encounter. Now he saw Elena as if for the first time. Shy, and of a lighter complexion than Nilda, she gave the impression of depending wholly on her friend—girlfriend or lover. He didn't care. He had no interest in either one of them.

Walter came home on Saturday after two, flung himself on his bed and fell asleep. His room was in darkness when he awoke. The inventory work of the past week, often late into the nights, had been exhausting; yet, he thought, it shouldn't have worn me down so much as to fall asleep in the middle of the afternoon. He groped for the slip of paper

Roswita had given him. It had remained in his coat pocket since the day before. Five o'clock on a Saturday afternoon, he hardly expected her to be at home.

He heard Nilda and Elena talking in the living room. Mrs. Nieves's telephone was on a table in the hall. Walter dialed Roswita's number.

"Felicia Napolitano," that smoky voice that had intrigued him the first time he heard it and stirred him deep inside. It still stirred him, but not in the same way.

"Hi, Felicia. It's Walter. Walter Hansen. We had a good time the other night. Say, is Roswita home?"

"I bet you had a good time. We could hear you having a good time. Yes, she's here. Just a sec, let me call her." He heard her, "Roswita, Walter on the phone."

Could she and What's-her-name really have heard us?

"Hi Walter. I thought you'd be calling yesterday. Still counting your nuts, I guess?" followed by a salvo of her frivolous laugh. "You coming over?"

"Stop it with the nuts, Roswita. It's not funny."

"I know. Six-inch hoses and rods and rubber sleeves— I like all that stuff. So, are you coming? No pun intended."

She can't help herself. A one-track mind. "You mean today, now?"

"Why not? I'm not doing anything. You can meet Claire, another one of those *Fotzenleckers*. Know what I mean? I am surrounded by them. Hold it. What, Felix? Oh, come on. I'm just kidding. All right, Walter, bring something to drink. I am sick of that Four Roses stuff. Not much left, anyway. A bottle of scotch, maybe. Old Smuggler is not too expensive."

"But I am hungry and tired."

141

"I'll get Chinese from around the corner on Astoria, okay?"

At the liquor store on Broadway, he bought a quart of Cutty Sark; it left him almost penniless. His overtime pay would not come until next payday. He took the subway to Roosevelt Avenue, then walked seven or eight blocks to save his precious tokens instead of taking the bus. There had been only one snowfall so far this winter, but now the streets were snow and ice-free and the cold air was invigorating.

Felicia opened the door for Walter. "Claire's asleep in her bedroom. She just returned from Europe. You won't be too loud, okay?"

Roswita joined them in the hall. "We are never loud, right Walter? Give me that and hang up your coat." She took the bag with the bottle of scotch from him. "Oh, Cutty Sark! Must have cost you a bundle. You want Chinese? I'll buy."

Walter did not get home that evening. He didn't get home the following two nights either. What will I tell Mrs. Nieves, he thought. He had promised to let her know in advance, so she wouldn't have to bother about his breakfast.

The New Year had begun. Tuesday, January 2, he called her in the morning before Paul came in. "Mrs. Nieves, I am so sorry. But something came up. Here at work. I told you about the inventory, right? Well, something had to be fixed. We worked all through the weekend, New Years and all. I didn't get out of here for three days."

"You couldn't come up with something better than that?" Roswita stood next to him at the payphone. "She can't be that gullible. You're a bad liar," she laughed. "You don't think she bought it, huh?"

"I don't think so. I don't think she believed a word I said."

"I would throw you out. We will have to find you another place."

"No, I think she likes me. She thinks of me as her son, she once told me."

"That will change. She can't possibly trust you anymore." Roswita thought for a moment. "Too bad you can't move in here. If Claire... no, she'll never leave. Felix and her, those two love birds..."

"Are the pilot and the steward downstairs *schwul*, too?"

"What? Are you kidding? No! They have girls there all the time, airport whores and stewardesses." And after a while, "You better be nice to your Mrs. Nieves. You might have to stay there until, until..."

Paul came in. "Good morning. Happy New Year!"

"Guten Morgen," Roswita said cheerfully in her broadest Saxon.

PART III
It will be great to be rich.

Chapter Thirteen

"**I** have an idea." Roswita leaned forward to turn off the television. "I have an idea, Walter. See if you like it."

They sat next to each other on the convertible couch in their East Thirty-fifth Street studio apartment. Roswita, after her job interview with Max Factor down the block, had stopped by the agent on the ground floor of the renovated brownstone. A month later Walter and Roswita moved into the apartment on the top floor.

"Yes," said Walter, "so what's this idea you have? By the way, I was watching that, but okay. You have an idea?"

"Listen. How about we, you and I, getting rich. I have this job now and…"

"You are a receptionist. How do you want to get rich?"

"Not just me. Us. I told you I have an idea. I won't be a receptionist for long. I will, listen to this, I will invent a perfume. I'll call it 'A Night with Roswita'. Something like that." She snuggled close to him. "You see, we will be rich, Walter. In the meantime you stay with AID. When Ernst Straub retires you'll get his job. You are already supervisor.

More money comes in. As soon as my perfume takes off you become my business manager. Should I keep my job with Max Factor? What do you think?"

"Oh, definitely keep the job."

"Yes. For now. But what do you think of my idea? Brilliant, huh?"

Walter had listened with only half an ear. He put his arm around her shoulder and pulled her to him. "You are brilliant. Now, your idea... It might need a little work. For example, don't you have to be a chemist, or a botanist, traveling to exotic places, finding fragrant plants? Know how to extract sap or essence and then to process it? Sure, your idea to get rich is brilliant, I just don't know..."

"Walter, listen to me. I don't have to know a thing. I figured it all out in my head. You have seen the little vials I brought home, haven't you? Samples? I also know where to get those odd-shaped flasks. Salesmen come in with catalogues all the time. Half ounce, quarter ounce..."

"And you will take the samples and, and..."

"No, not just like that! That would be dumb. I will mix different scents and come up with a new, exciting perfume. That's what is so brilliant about my idea. Get it? Do you?"

He got it all right. From the start, when he first met her, he knew she was... well, crazy. Half crazy, at least. But he liked her carefree attitude, her bold, unabashed way of talking in that comical Saxon accent, and that semi-transparent summer dress she wore the day Walter came to AID looking for a job. Now, two years later, sitting on the couch in front of the television set she had just turned off, Roswita revealed this new side of her. Criminal? Perhaps not. Fraudulent? Could be. Surely conniving.

"A lot of details to be worked out," he said. "For one thing, the supply. Then, how would you market it?"

"I didn't say it was perfect. Brilliant, though, you must admit. Oh, Walter, it will be great to be rich."

Walter has never been rich, not even close. His father let him fend for himself when he sent him to Frankfurt to learn the fur business. Later, in Vienna, he barely kept his head above water. In New York he was lucky to find a job within a few days after his arrival, but at sixty-five dollars a week, even a postage stamp was a luxury he couldn't afford.

Walter was in his second year at AID when Paul Kempowski quit, and he got the supervisor job. Hundred and twenty-five dollars gave him the feeling he was slowly getting rich, but that feeling didn't last. His needs became greater: a new suit, a pair of shoes, once or twice a month eating out in a restaurant.

Then he still lived at Mrs. Nieves's rooming house and more often he had to tell her, "No breakfast for me tomorrow, Mrs. Nieves. I won't be coming home tonight." Since that first Christmas in New York, when he had stayed over at Roswita's place, his life changed. Soon some of his clothes found a place in her closet. Her roommates, Felicia and Claire, sometimes saw Walter in the mornings rushing out of the apartment. They didn't have any objections; people were constantly coming and leaving.

The apartment Roswita, Felicia and Claire rented was on the top floor. A male flight attendant and a co-pilot lived on the second floor. There were always parties, and often it wasn't clear who lived there and who didn't. On the ground floor, besides the garage where Felicia Napolitano stored her

147

convertible Beetle, there were a utility room and a small studio, which the landlady occupied.

"Miss Napolitano," the elderly, widowed landlady addressed Felicia who had just backed her car into the garage. "The neighbors asked me about all the comings and goings of young men and women, the music, the parties. I am not complaining, Miss Napolitano, it's just… They seem to be concerned about what's going on. I rented the apartment to you and Miss Peschel and the other young woman, but now I myself sometimes don't know who lives there. I'll also have to talk to the two gentlemen on the second floor. You know, people are not used to that in this neighborhood."

"Oh, ma'am, don't worry. There's really nothing going on. You see, we work for the airlines and we have irregular schedules. That's why all this coming and going."

That, of course, was a vague answer; it confused the lady even more and she didn't know how to respond. "Yes, ah, okay, all right then, that must be it, I mean, I don't know. I am just telling you what the neighbors say. But you explained it, so, yes, it must be difficult, with the schedules and all. If you could, perhaps, you know, keep it… well, respectable. And I know, you do. I only mention it because, you know, the neighbors…"

Felicia patted the old lady lightly on the shoulder. "I understand, so don't you worry."

"Oh, I don't. You are nice tenants. I like it when the young people have some fun. It's the neighbors, you know."

"Yes, I know. The neighbors." Felicia smiled at her, gave her shoulder a little squeeze and then turned to go upstairs. At the apartment door she met Roswita and Walter who were just leaving.

"We're going out," said Roswita. "Want to come with us?"

"No, I just got back from Europe. Listen, Roxy, I had a chat with the landlady. The neighbors are talking, she told me," and to Walter, "Are you coming back tonight?"

Walter didn't like the way that sounded. "I am going home. We're just going somewhere to eat, then I'm going home."

"What's going on?" Roswita asked sharply. "Felix, what did you tell her? What did she complain about? She thinks we are running a whorehouse here? She can't hear us upstairs. Must be about those two below us. What did you say? Is she going to throw us out? Are we in trouble?"

"No, no. All she said was the neighbors are talking."

That evening, Walter went home but Roswita had an argument with Felicia. "What about Megan, huh? You sleep with her when Claire is not here. Now suddenly you tell me, Walter can't come here anymore?"

"I didn't say that. The woman said, the neighbors noticed people coming and going all the time. We have to cool it, is all I'm saying."

"You said specifically to Walter, 'are you coming back tonight?' I know what you meant by that."

"I can't talk to you when you get like this."

The argument grew more heated. "You want me out?" Roswita hurled at her. "Then why don't you just say so?" She threw her head back. "You know, I've had it. You and Claire, you and Megan, Megan and Claire, or whatever—that's okay. But me and Walter, that's not okay."

That was only the beginning. Now that Paul Kempowski was no longer there and Walter had been promoted to supervisor, it became more difficult for Roswita and Walter to keep their affair secret. Company policy did not condone inter-office relationships. Ernst Straub warned her, "better for you to quit before you get fired."

The personnel manager called Roswita in. "Miss Peschel, we are aware of your, eh, liaison with, eh, another employee. It's against company rules. I recommend you to end that, eh, liaison or look for employment elsewhere. This is a warning, but you must end it immediately."

Faced with this dilemma, Roswita began to search for a job and she was thrilled to be accepted by the cosmetics company of Max Factor. At the reception desk in the liberal, glamorous atmosphere, at the high end of style and fashion, she found herself in a different world.

The brilliant idea of creating a perfume came to her the first week at Max Factor. "It will be great to be rich, Walter," she repeated. "What do you say? Aren't you excited? We will have a car, a boat, go on vacation in exotic places, mingle with famous people. I already met with models, TV producers, agents and…"

"You met these people? What do you mean, you met them?"

"Walter, I am the first one they see when they come in. Yesterday, Bruno came in for the second time since I started. I think he just wanted to talk to me."

"Bruno? That's his name? Who is he? A big shot of some sort? What did he want to talk about?"

"Oh, it's nothing like that. He's the agent for those fancy crystal flasks, the makeup containers with the mirrors, lipstick tubes and all that stuff. Real pretty things women like to carry in their purses. You wouldn't know."

"So, he's a salesman. Why did he want to talk to you? Did he ask you out?"

"No, Walter. It's not like that. He just talked. He wants to go into business by himself. Cosmetics, he said. He has lots of connections, he told me."

"And that gave you the idea with the perfume. Did he come up with the name for it, 'A Night with Roswita'?" Walter reached out to turn the TV on again. "You'd better get that out of your head. You can't just steal perfume, mix it up and sell it in Bruno's bottles, if that's the brilliant idea you have."

"I thought of 'A Night with Roswita'. Don't you like it? And, Walter, it's not stealing, it's free samples. Next time I see Bruno I'll ask him some more questions."

"Regardless, I think this Bruno type is putting ideas into your head. You'd better be careful. I don't like any of it." The program he had been watching was over and he turned the set off.

The last time he had dropped in at Bernhard Goldsmith's office was at least six months ago, shortly after his promotion to supervisor at AID, to let him know that he was doing well. I really should call more often, Walter thought. After all, he has been essential in getting me started in New York.

In the morning on his way to work, he had already forgotten that he should make a courtesy call not only to Mister Goldsmith, but also to Joe and Gerda Chang. The next time Walter was reminded that he owed the Changs a call was weeks later. Roswita sat on the couch, a drink in front of her on the coffee table. She usually came home from work earlier than Walter—Max Factor was just down the block; what was unusual was that she had a drink by herself, before Walter came home.

"Something to celebrate?" he asked as he hung up his coat in the closet.

"They arrested Bruno," she said.

Walter joined her on the couch. "The cosmetics guy?"

"Accessories, Walter, accessories. Now I can't get the flasks, the bottles I need for my enterprise. It's all falling apart. A new salesman came in, and I don't like him. He told me Bruno faces a lot of charges."

Walter let out his breath. It was a breath of relief. "Just before you were getting involved with him and his scams. They would be hauling your ass off to jail, too. So, what's with the long face? I told you…"

"I thought he was a nice guy, trying to make a living. He was a nice guy, trying to make a living, but he got into bad company. Counterfeit Gucci and Fendi stuff, cheap imitations, fake prescription drugs from China or some place. I liked him." She sipped her drink. "This new character, pretending to be a real business type, he thinks he's better than Bruno, and I don't like him."

"Roswita, you don't have to like everybody."

"I know. I have to pull myself together. Walter, what are we going to do to get rich?" She held up her empty glass. "Fill this up for me and get yourself a drink, will you, Walter? It's the scotch. We need a fresh bottle."

Walter came back to the couch with two glasses and didn't say anything.

Then she came out with something that must have been in her head since they arrested Bruno. "What about your friends, that couple in New Brunswick or some place? They are in the drug or cosmetics business, right? Maybe I can get the flasks..."

"Roswita, what are you saying? Are you insane? He is a chemist, a scientist, in legitimate pharmaceutical business. Bristol-Myers. Forget the flasks, forget the whole idea," and under his breath, "it was a stupid idea to begin with."

"You have seen all the sample vials, right? What am I going to do with all that perfume?"

"Use it. Not all at once, though," he chuckled.

A day later, Roswita brought home a dozen tiny glass dishes and set them out on the kitchen counter. Breaking open the vials, she began to experiment, mixing drops of one scent with that of another. Soon all the dishes had small puddles of strong and fragrant aromas.

That evening Walter entered the apartment to what he thought smelled like a Hawaiian whorehouse. "What the hell... Roswita!" His nostrils stung from the biting, sweet smell. "Roswita, are you okay?"

"I have a headache and I am dizzy. I had to lie down."

"You have to get out of here. I'll get you a sweater. We can't stay here another minute. How come you didn't pass out? This nonsense has to stop. You are obsessed with this. Come on, you need fresh air."

She barely made it with Walter's help to the park in front of their building where they sat down on a bench. Quickly the fresh air cleared her head.

"I turned the fans on in the bathroom and in the kitchen," said Walter, "but that may not be enough."

153

"You think we can go back in and sleep with the windows open?"

"I should have thrown everything down the garbage chute."

"Nooo! Walter, maybe we can crash with Felicia and Claire tonight. In the apartment we'd end up dead in the morning."

Felicia was away on a flight to Zurich. Roswita convinced Claire that it was an emergency. "We don't know what to do, Claire. They fumigated the building."

The following evening they returned to their apartment. The dishes were all empty and dry; there was only a hint of musty sweetness still hanging in the air.

Roswita sat down and cried. "It's gone. It's all gone. My dream… evaporated."

The fans in the kitchen and the bathroom were still running. Walter turned them off and opened the windows to let the fresh air in. What can I say to her? It will pass. She wanted to get perfume bottles from Joe Chang, an insane idea. Now she had nothing to put in them. Good. But, anyway, I have to give Gerda a call. Her and Goldsmith. I don't have to talk to Joe.

"Hello Gerda! Walter. How are you? I know, it's been a long time. Always something, you know."

She said, she had called Mrs. Nieves. "You moved out, she told me. Where to, Walter?"

"Yes, I make a little more money now as supervisor. I can't afford it by myself, so I have a roommate. It's on Thirty-fifth Street, between First and Second."

"That's great."

"How is Joe? And Mister Goldsmith? Please give them my regards. I just called to say hello. Gotta get back to work. Hmm? Yes, we'll get together. Soon. I'll call you. No, I don't have a phone yet."

Ooooh, that was awkward. But it will carry me over for a few months.

He had sent his mother a note after he moved out of Mrs. Nieves's boarding home to give them his new address. He did not mention Roswita. His mother wrote, *supervisor, is that something like* Meister? *Now that you have your own apartment I can come and visit you. Your father is not interested. He still does not like that you broke with the tradition of his family. Write to me when is a good time to come to New York.*

Never, he thought. There's never a good time. Roswita hasn't even mentioned her parents. He knew so little about her. Perhaps better that way, he thought, and did not tell her of his mother's letter.

Roswita quickly recovered from the loss of her unlikely business and Walter convinced her that it was a bad idea.

"I spoke to one of the models the other day. She wants me to get an interview with her agent. I have such pretty hands, she told me. I always thought it was my hair they could use in an advertisement, but no, she said, my hands. What do you think?"

"I think you have pretty hands and pretty hair."

"Oh, thank you, Walter. You really mean it?"

"Of course I mean it," he said quite earnestly. "Let me see. Long, slim fingers, a slender hand, no fat and no protruding veins. Nice. For nail polish or fake nail ads. What do they call that? A hand job? You're good at a hand job, I mean…"

She responded to the double entendre with her provocative, borderline vulgar laugh and punched him hard on the shoulder. He pushed back, she resisted and for the next hour and a half, they wriggled and squirmed in exquisite ecstasy on the floor.

The week after Walter had taken over Paul's job as supervisor, Ernst Straub hired a young man to assist in the tiresome inventory control of the thousands of automotive parts and accessories. Gerhard, a distant relative of Straub, had just arrived from Germany. At eighteen and fresh out of high school in Stuttgart, he spoke fairly good English, the way they teach it in German schools. Walter had no difficulty showing him the ropes and Gerhard quickly got the hang of it.

"Mister Hansen, may I ask you something?"

"Yes, what is it? And, call me Walter. We go by first names here. Only Mister Straub is Mister Straub."

"All right then, Walter, thank you. As you know, I stay at my uncle's, that is Mister Straub's house. Well, he is a cousin of my father and I call him Onkel Ernst. But he told me, here at work it had to be Mister Straub."

"Uh-huh, so?"

"Well, I would rather live by myself and my uncle, Mister Straub, also says this is just temporary. He said the other day something about going back to Germany, but I don't know."

"Oh yeah? He said that?"

"Ah, I think I shouldn't have told you."

"That's okay. I won't say anything. About a place... Let me think about it."

Walter's room at Mrs. Nieves's boarding house had remained unoccupied since he moved out. For nearly three months, Nilda Ponce and Elena were the only boarders, and Mrs. Nieves was delighted when Walter introduced Gerhard to her. She took the polite and friendly young man in.

For some time there had been rumors that Ernst Straub contemplated an early retirement and return to Germany. That could open a new opportunity for Walter, but his chances for such a big step up the ladder were slim just six months after his promotion to supervisor. He had been lucky; he would still be the underpaid inventory clerk if Paul Kempowski had not moved on to a better job elsewhere, after nearly five years with AID. Since the company did not hire anyone for the position vacated by Roswita, Walter essentially filled the role of secretary to Mister Straub, in addition to his job as supervisor in inventory control.

"Straub's not even sixty, I think," said Roswita. "I never heard him talking about retiring."

"Neither did I, but Franz seems to know something and now Gerhard... If that's true, I am screwed. They won't give me his job. I have less than three years with the company, and they can't move Gerhard up to take my job. He's too young and doesn't know enough yet."

"Walter, what will happen to our plan to get rich?"

"Rich? Your plan, you mean. First of all, it's not official that Straub will retire any time soon. Second, they probably won't make me manager. And third, if they did, even that would not make us rich. For now, we have trouble making the rent. I told you the apartment is too expensive for us."

"Helen Rossi got me that interview with her agent, but it will take time until I make any money as a hand model—if they take me."

"Helen Rossi? The model? What does she model? Hands?"

"Teeth. She models teeth. Well, she has a nice smile. She always comes in for her lipsticks. Samples, you know. She doesn't make much money yet either. Fifty dollars a shot. Once she made seven hundred a week, she told me."

"So, when's your interview? Do you have to sleep with the agent? Isn't that how it goes?"

"I might have to. Is that a problem?" She was completely sincere. "I mean, would you mind?"

"Oh no, of course not," he mocked her. "Just tell him to wear a condom."

"I'll go Tuesday after work. By the way, the agent is a woman."

"Ah, that's different."

"How so? How is that different? Except for the condom, I mean. No place to put it." Then she added sheepishly, "I have some experience, you know."

"You do? Tell me."

"Oh, it's nothing, really. Felicia and I... Once. We had a lot to drink. It was good, but I didn't really like it."

"Hm. Felicia, huh? She's a wild one. Damn good looking too, and that voice..."

"Walter, she doesn't do guys. You can take your mind off her."

158

On Tuesday night, Roswita came home from the upper Westside after midnight. Walter had already pulled out the couch and was in bed. "How did it go?" he asked.

"It was exhausting. Exhausting, I say! The interview was quick. Then she sent me to the studio next door. The photographer took a hundred photos. Not one of me, it's all about my hands. Holding a plastic cheeseburger, a can of soda, dipping them into a jar of lotion, squeezing a lemon... Oh yeah, and opening a box of chocolates. Over and over again. And those were just tests. They call it body parts modeling in the business."

"So, did you get the job?" He interrupted.

"Then back to the agent. She's an old woman. It was already eleven o'clock. She told me, she'll let me know. They will develop the pictures and study them. Then the subway. It's creepy at night."

"What did they say about your hands? Body parts, huh?"

"The photographer said I should wear gloves for everything I do. I have to get a manicure at least every other week. Something about my cuticles. I see nothing wrong with them. He's a grouch and a fag. Wears corduroy. What a nerd."

"Manicure? Let me see."

"They are sore, Walter. Don't look at them. Especially the right. The right did most of the work. I should soak them in warm water and Epsom salt. Do we have any Epsom salt? What is Epsom salt? Do we have any? Oh, I am so tired. I'll just go to bed. Have you eaten? I haven't. But I'm not hungry. Only thirsty. Make me a scotch. I'll be just a minute." She went to the bathroom, undressed and then came to bed. He had her drink ready. "Thank you, Walter. I didn't know body parts modeling was so hard."

Chapter Fourteen

Ernst Straub did not announce his decision to retire until the following summer. Walter, now thirty-two years old, applied for promotion to manager and in the fall he took over the position Straub vacated. The company, still in the no-hiring mode, did not grant him a secretary, but had to employ a young girl to work with Gerhard in inventory control. Walter felt well qualified to handle his new job; however, the workload often made it necessary for him to remain at his desk until six or seven in the evening.

He took home four hundred dollars every other Friday—far less than they had paid Straub—but it was the year 1962, and four hundred bucks no longer got him as far as it used to. Roswita had an occasional body parts job that added fifty to their income, but her expenses had doubled, with make-up, manicures and wardrobe to keep up with other models.

"I am a model now, Walter. I have to look the part. My photographer said so."

Walter countered, "Yeah, a parts model. Your parts have to look the part."

She did not respond to his quibble. Instead, after a moment, she came out with, "He has a sailboat. You are a sailor, right? You told me. I have never been on a boat."

"Who? The photographer?"

"Stephan's his name. Stephan Polish or something, with an itch at the end. But he's a nerd. Are all sailors such nerds? I am sure he's queer, too. I know, you are not a nerd and you're not a queer." With her frivolous laugh she added, "That I know."

"So, why are you telling me this? You want to go sailing with a nerd who's also a homo?" The mention of a sailboat got his attention. He had not been in a boat since that cruise around Denmark, some ten years before. Is it that long? He had not thought about it; now suddenly he felt the yearning for a boat. "I'd love to go sailing. Is he really such a nerd? And queer? What kind of a boat? And where…"

"You ask me all these questions. I don't know. Helen told me. She and her boyfriend once went with him. What do I know? A boat, with sails, I guess, in the water."

"Can't you ask him?"

"I don't know. I have to run, Walter. Is my hair all right? I hope he likes my hands today. We really should get that Epsom salt. He's gonna ask me."

Since Roswita got into body parts modeling, Walter spent more Saturdays alone and he didn't like it. He wished he had a car to be independent, but his budget did not yet allow such luxury. Roswita spent most of her money on herself. Would she ever break into the world of high fashion? She had the looks—tall, slender, long legs, good hair. This Stephan something or other, he specializes in body parts. Nothing but body parts. Is he really homosexual? Or does she just say that? I have to get out of here.

He zipped his down jacket up to his chin and strolled through the park adjacent to the United Nations building. A brisk wind came across the East River on this cold Saturday morning in late fall. A tug struggled against the current, pulling a string of barges up river. Sailboats were probably out of the water for the approaching winter, he thought. Where might Stephan store his boat? Roswita didn't know. Perhaps in the spring we could go sailing with him, but spring is a long time off.

Walter left the park, walked along Forty-second Street to Lexington Avenue and entered Horn & Hardart. The automated vending machines still fascinated him. He chose a hamburger and a slice of apple pie. Seated at the window, he absentmindedly watched people hurrying by, while others waited for the green light to cross the busy avenue.

A boat, he daydreamed. Perhaps a small sailboat. There is water all around here. The Hudson, the East River, Long Island Sound. Would Roswita like it? He pictured her on his boat, in white pants, or in the summer in a bikini, sunburned, hair tousled in the wind, sunglasses.

He left the restaurant and crossed over to Fifth Avenue. The sun had come out but did not warm the air in the gorge between the skyscrapers. The lions guarding the steps to the library failed to call his attention as he continued to mull over the prospect of some day having a boat. A small one. How expensive could it be? But the upkeep, and where to store it... Stop dreaming, he told himself. But, no. Keep on dreaming. Some day, some day. If I want it strongly enough, it might happen. Some day.

Roswita had come home already and was in the shower. "How was it?" he asked, pulling the curtain aside a little at one end. "Did you have a good session?"

"It was okay. Jewelry. Now, let me finish here."

"Did you ask him about his boat? I've been thinking…"

"Walter, let me finish. I'll be out in two seconds. What boat? No, I didn't ask him. What's this about a boat all of a sudden?"

He hung his jacket in the closet and then sat on the couch.

She came out of the shower, a towel wrapped intricately around her hair, another covering her upper body to the waist. "I had these gorgeous rings on my fingers, for a catalogue of De Beers. I would get seventy five for today, Mrs. Dubois told me."

"Mrs. Dubois?"

"The agent." Roswita stood in front of him, half naked. He didn't seem to notice.

"I've been thinking. Wouldn't you like to have a boat? Maybe on the Hudson? We could sail into the bay, by the Statue of Liberty, and up to the George Washington Bridge, anchor somewhere overnight under the Palisades. In the summer…"

"Walter, I stand here, naked, and you talk about a boat?"

"Come here, you. I am sorry. You look delicious." He reached out and pulled her next to him onto the couch.

In the weeks that followed, his thoughts centered on having a boat. He couldn't get it out of his head. At work, parts catalogues were full of accessories that could be used on a boat. In the warehouse, coils of wire cables became shrouds and stays in his mind. Bulbs were for navigation lights, tires reminded him of fenders as used on tugboats. Repair kits, fasteners, clamps and hoses, canvas intended for seat covers or convertible tops, even packing material—he saw it all as useful on his future boat.

He left the office after working late one night as the cleaning crew came in. Parked at the curb stood a '51 Mercury. He had seen the exact model the first time in Frankfurt. Leo Reichenberg's car. A dream car, he had called it. Walter walked around it. He could not see it very well there in the street, poorly illuminated by a distant street light, but he saw it was green, just like Leo Reichenberg's. On the windshield was a For Sale sign. He went back into the office. "Anybody know whose car that is out there? The Mercury?"

The foreman of the cleaning crew stopped his vacuum cleaner. "She's mine."

"You're selling it? It's twelve years old. What do you want for it?"

"She's a fifty-one. Runs good. Noth'n wrong with her. You interested?"

"That's almost twelve. Interested? Maybe. How much? What's your name?"

"Leroy. Two fifty."

"I am Walter. One fifty. I'd have to see it in daylight. Can you come early tomorrow evening?"

"Two hundred. I can come by five tomorrow, okay?"

Once, last summer, Walter had rented a car, right after he got his driver license. He drove with Roswita out of the city across the George Washington Bridge and up the Palisades Parkway to Bear Mountain. Very insecure at first in city traffic, he gained confidence on the Parkway. He had not driven since. The novelty of owning a car made his heart beat a little faster.

He justified his need for a car. If I want a boat, I have to have a car. No question about it. But the money... Roswita, I'm sure she can chip in a little.

Leroy showed up the following afternoon. "Wanna take her for a spin around the block? She's all warmed up."

It was still light enough for Walter to see some rust under the doorframe, but he discovered no dents or scratches. Leroy lifted the hood. "V-Eight," he said, "overdrive, new transmission couple o' years ago. Needs an oil change, that's all."

Walter looked at the tires; they looked okay. "Spare?" he asked.

"In the trunk, never used. Tools, too. Two hundred and she's yours."

Walter opened the door. "Seats look worn. There's a tear in the fabric of the driver seat. I need to buy seat covers. One fifty. How does that sound?"

"Oh, man, I can't do it. Tell you what, gimme one seventy-five."

"Deal," said Walter. They shook hands. Walter got behind the wheel and Leroy, in the seat beside him, handed him the key.

"The key goes here. Starter button's on the left of the steering wheel. Turn the key, step on the clutch and press the button. See? She starts right up. Now, you know how to drive, right?" The car lurched forward. "Take it easy, man. That's a powerful engine."

Back in front of the building, Walter asked, "Got the title on you? And the registration? I have the money at my desk."

Done with the formalities, Walter had ahead of him the exciting but difficult task of informing Roswita. Not that she would object to his spontaneous action; that was not the problem. The problem was to come up with the money for the insurance.

He drove his dream car into Manhattan and parked it under the elevated East River Drive, a block from home. He had seen cars parked there, in a dirty, muddy lot. It did not seem very safe, but who would steal a twelve-years old car?

"Roswita, I want to show you something. Get a sweater. Come on."

"What? You bought a boat?"

"No. Come on, you'll see."

They crossed First Avenue and entered the dark, eerie lot, sidestepping puddles between cars. Roswita shivered. "Where are you taking me? This is creepy."

He stopped in front of the Mercury. "What do you think, huh?"

"What is it? I can't see." There was only the glimmer of some naked bulbs hanging from the highway above them, traffic noise adding to the sinister sensation this place gave her. "You bought a car?"

"Not just a car. A dream car! '51 Mercury, V-Eight, overdrive, the works. Runs like a charm. What do you say?"

At first, she was speechless. Then, when they sat in a Thirty-fourth-Street diner, "You bought us a car. Oh, Walter, that's wonderful. Can we afford it?"

"There is one thing. I need to get the registration. That's okay, but the insurance will cost more than the car. The guy said it's gonna be at least two hundred for the first year. I don't have it."

"Two hundred?" She examined her mud-encrusted shoes. "You want me to…"

"Can you? I have to do that tomorrow morning. There is an insurance agency across the street. See the sign?" *Insurance for Less*, a neon sign flashed in a shop window.

On Saturday they took the first ride in their car, crossed the Brooklyn Bridge, drove along Flatbush Avenue all the way out to Sheepshead Bay. They looked at boats.

"That's the real purpose of the car, Roswita. You think I have forgotten about the boat? No. First the car, then the boat. How else? We need a car to get to the boat."

"Walter, listen to me. We are broke. You hear me? Broke, I say. Mrs. Dubois has not called me for almost a month. I had to skip my manicure this week. Stephan will not like it, so I'm not telling him."

"My Christmas bonus is due in three weeks."

"I don't think they'll give us one. I heard rumors. Or a very small one."

Walter's Christmas bonus was generous. He gave Roswita half of the insurance money back. "Here's a hundred-ten dollars. Merry Christmas! I bought a set of seat covers. Got a discount, you know. We put'em on tomorrow morning."

Then, in mid-January, Mrs. Dubois had a surprise for Roswita. "I'll send you to Puerto Rico for a photo shoot on the beach," she told her. "You fly on Wednesday, come back Friday. It's for a travel magazine. I already talked to your boss at Max Factor."

Roswita told Walter the moment he came home in the evening. "Seven hundred dollars, all expenses paid." She hugged him tightly. "First time more than just my hands. All of me, Walter, or I don't know how much."

"You need new clothes? A bikini? Stuff like that?"

"Nothing. I mean, they have all that for me. And the photographer, Renaldo's his name. First name, last name—I don't know. I will meet him there."

Was this the break they had been waiting for?

Roswita returned from Puerto Rico in the early morning hours of Saturday. "Are you awake, Walter? I am exhausted, but invigorated. The sun, the beach, last night at a club... We stayed at the cottages outside San Juan. There were others there. Models, a PR man and agents. Renaldo is Italian. I liked him."

Walter propped himself up on the elbows. "Did he like you, too?"

"I think so. Oh, yes, definitely." She gave him a quick kiss. "I'll just go in the shower, then I come to bed."

Fully awake now, he considered her new career—if it should become a career. She would probably have to travel, be away for any length of time. London, Paris …

From the open bathroom door, over the noise of the hair dryer, she called out to him. "I hope the pictures came out all right. There are dozens. They'll choose only one or two of them. Renaldo said I should go to modeling school. But that's expensive. What do you think?"

"I don't know. What do you think?"

"I think I should go." She turned the hair dryer off. The apartment was cold and she hurried to get under the comforter with Walter.

They cuddled. "Hmm," she cooed close to his ear. "You like this? Good, huh?"

"Uh-huh. Good. Oh, ah, there. Yes. That's good. Oh, this is new. Now let me…"

"No, wait. There's more." How and where she touched him, kissed him—a whole new repertoire.

"Oooh, ah, Roswita…"

"Oooh, ah, Renal… ah, Walter…"

When it was over, they were quiet for a long moment. Their breathing returned to normal.

"Roswita," he began. "What… You said…"

"I am sorry, Walter. We'd been drinking. He came to my cabana. One thing led to another. It didn't mean anything. I'll never see him again. Probably."

They stayed glued together, but said no more. She waited for a response from him, but he remained quiet. I knew this would happen, he reflected. It was understood from the start. I shouldn't let it bother me.

"Were there others?" he asked after a while. "I mean since we live together?"

"Let me think. Since we moved here? No, not that I recall. Bruno—remember him? The guy they put in jail? He wanted to, but I didn't like him that way. So, no."

He knew she was truthful. "That's good." He disentangled himself from her and went in to take a shower. Should I look elsewhere too, for fun and recreation? He pondered, but then concluded that he didn't really want to. When he returned to bed, Roswita was asleep.

Chapter Fifteen

On a crisp, clear spring morning, Walter drove to Stony Point on the Hudson. He had asked Gerhard to accompany him on his mission. "I have to pick something up this Saturday. I could use your help," he told him. Gerhard was happy to do his boss a favor and did not ask for what his help was wanted.

Out of the city, driving north on the Parkway, Walter talked about his sailing adventure when he was just out of high school. "Have you ever had a boat, Gerhard?"

"Oh, yes. I had a canoe. There was a lake near where we lived. Me and my friends had a little cottage. We spent weekends there."

"But a sailboat?"

"No. I have never sailed."

"Well, I bought a boat. It's only ten feet. It fits on top of the car. I brought rope to tie it down. That's what I want you to help me with."

"A boat? A sailboat?"

"Yes." They stopped at the dealer, and there it was, in the shed, ready for pick-up. The turquoise fiberglass hull, the mast, centerboard and rudder, the sails in a blue canvas bag. Two men helped lift the boat onto the roof of the car, secure it with rope and then they tied the mast and boom along the passenger side.

Careful not to upset his precious cargo, Walter drove slowly south on 9W. He had previously rented a slip at a small marina in Upper Nyack, a single dock with slips for half a dozen boats. *Koenig's Marina*, read a sign nailed to the gate that led to a yard and a rustic shed.

"That's the boat?" Burly Jim Koenig, dressed in baggy denim overalls, scratched his head. "I don't know what to charge you for that. Tell you what: we bring her in close where it's too shallow for bigger boats. Then it's thirty-five a month, okay? Can't charge you more for that."

Jim helped with the unloading. They carried the boat to the water's edge and let it slide from the narrow, gravelly beach into its predestined element.

Barefoot, and pant's legs rolled up, Walter and Gerhard secured the boat in the slip, then fitted the centerboard and the rudder and stepped the mast.

"Thank you, Gerhard. You will be one of the first to sail with me, after I try her out a few times. If you like."

Throughout the winter months, Walter had studied sailing magazines, searching for a boat he might be able to afford. He drove Roswita crazy with his obsession.

"There's nothing here. They are all too expensive. I have to go smaller, but I want one with two sails, you know, main and jib."

"I don't know what you are talking about."

He leafed through a catalogue. "These are manufacturers. New boats. There are pictures. See?"

"Yeah, I see, but I still don't know what you're talking about."

"Roswita, what about this one? It has what I want. Ten feet—that small?" He scanned the particulars listed in the advertisement. "Let me call them up."

"It's Sunday."

"Oh, yeah," he realized. "Roswita, I might have to take a day off next week. This one is in Stony Point, up the Hudson."

And that is what he did. He drove to Stony Point, less than an hour north of the George Washington Bridge, and made a down payment on an O'Day Sprite, ready to be delivered in three-weeks time.

When Walter on that cold Saturday returned from Stony Point and Koenig's Marina in Upper Nyack, Roswita was not home. All afternoon he waited with growing impatience to tell her the news. "We are the owners of a sailboat, Roswita," he practiced. No, he mused, more subtle. "You know what I did this morning?" No, she knows I was going to look at boats. What she doesn't know is that I already bought one. How about this, "Roswita, what would be a good name for a boat? You know, the one I just bought?" Oh, yeah, that would knock her right out of her high heels. What takes her so long? Her classes were from one to four. She should have been here by five.

Roswita had begun three months of private lessons given by a professor of the Fashion Institute of Technology. Mrs. Dubois had recommended her and agreed to advance the hefty enrollment fee. At the end of the course, she would receive a certificate—short of a degree, but still valuable because of the professor's association with the prestigious New York school. Already her face had appeared in various ads in trade magazines, but so far no full figure photo. Stephan promised to get her picture on the city buses for an ad of the *New York Times* that would pay well. As soon as she had her certificate, Roswita would quit her job at Max Factor.

At seven, Walter heard giggling outside before the key turned the lock. Roswita pushed a tall girl with raven hair and a dazzling smile through the opening door.

"Walter, you are home! I thought you might be out. You don't like to be at home alone. This is Helen Rossi. We had a few drinks after class."

Walter turned the TV off and stood up. "Nice, ah, nice meeting you," he stumbled, bedazzled by the stunning apparition before him. "Roswita told me about you." He took her cool hand.

"Take your coat off, Helen," said Roswita. "Walter, you have a drink for us?"

"Sure." Now, how can I give her my news? Better wait until later. But then she might be too drunk.

With their drinks in hand, they stood in the middle of the room, Roswita and Helen laughing about some nonsense. Walter raised his glass. "A toast to the boat I just bought!" In the silence that followed, he said, "What? You don't believe me? Roswita, we talked about this. It's the tiny sloop I showed you in the catalogue weeks ago."

Roswita plumped down on the couch. "Helen, you believe this man? He goes and buys a boat—just like that."

"A boat?" asked Helen.

"Yes, listen, it's the ten-foot O'Day. Real small. No big deal. We can try it out tomorrow. Maiden voyage. If it's not too cold. What do you say, Roswita? But we should christen it first."

"O'Day? I say, oh boy."

"That's a good name: Oh Boy!" Helen clinked glasses with Roswita who still was incredulous. "Or Old Boy."

"Walter, boats cost at least, what? Thousands? How do you want to pay for it?"

"It's all paid. Nine hundred dollars. It's a tiny, open boat, like a dinghy, but with a mast and sails. You can see it tomorrow. Come on, Roswita. Cheer up!"

"The money... Where..."

"I had some stashed away. I have planned this for a long time, you know. Then I saw this ad last month. I showed it to you, remember? Aren't you happy?"

"Okay, so now we have a boat. Let me get this straight: it is small, very small; it has sails and a mast and I can see it tomorrow. Are you crazy?"

Helen put an arm around Roswita. "Come on, Roxy. I think it's great."

"Roxy...that's the name," Walter hit his forehead with a flat palm. "Roxy! We will christen her Roxy. Thanks, Helen."

On the sunny but cold Sunday morning they were on their way to Upper Nyack. "That Helen... Man, isn't she something?"

"Walter, you can get your mind off her. It's not gonna happen. She's practically engaged to her boyfriend."

"I don't mean that. But isn't she great? She came up with the name."

"Don't give me that. I know what you mean. Go ahead, I don't care, but it's not gonna happen. And, by the way, she didn't come up with the name. She just said..."

"Oh, all right." They came to the tollbooth, Walter threw the coins into the basket and then they continued northward. "But, really… You wouldn't mind?"

"I did this thing with Renaldo. What can I say?"

Forty-five minutes later they stopped at the gate to Koenig's Marina. "Here we are." He led Roswita onto the dock that protruded from the yard over the grimy narrow beach that now, at high tide, was under water.

A couple of boats rested in their slips. "Which one is yours?" she asked.

"Ours, Roswita, ours. Yours and mine. The first one."

"This is it? Nine hundred dollars?" She looked it over. "But it is cute, Walter. I like it. I just thought it would be a little bigger. How do I get on?"

Walter stepped down into the boat, then held his hand out. "Come on, step in the middle." The boat tilted from side to side. "Careful. Here, sit on the thwart. Now, let me show you a few things. This is called the centerboard, that's the tiller. The shrouds…"

"Walter, I am cold. Can you tell me all about it some other time?"

He helped her back onto the dock. "Yeah, all right. I am a little cold, too. Anyway, we can't go sailing today. We have to buy a few more things, but it so happens, I'm out of cash. What I had left went to Jim for the docking fee."

"Can't help you there. I am paying Mrs. Dubois back for the tuition. What else do you need? I thought the boat was complete."

"Life vests; it's the law. We need a little flag. And an anchor, for overnight, you know. And the letters R-O-X-Y, to put on the transom. Aren't you proud, she's named after you?"

176

"Yeah, sure. Let's get out of here. I am freezing."

Roswita's career was on an upswing, but she still brought home little more than her salary from Max Factor; most of her income from magazine ads went to repay Mrs. Dubois.

The days as a mere hands model were behind her. The course with the FIT professor ended in May. She now had a certificate that entitled her to call herself a professional model—a photo model, not a runway model. Since the beginning of April her picture rode on the sides of New York City buses. *I read the Classifieds in the New York Times,* she says, lying in tight jeans on a living room carpet. With luck, Stephan told her, she might some day get a part in a TV commercial.

Walter, as manager, received his pay at the end of every month. He had to wait two weeks to buy the accessories for the boat. Once, when Roswita was out all day taking pictures in New Jersey, he moved the boat out of the slip, put up the sails and, pushing along the other boats, got into open water. He immediately realized he should have a paddle to maneuver in and out of the slip. A light wind took him across the wide river, almost to Tarrytown on the other side, when it began to rain and the wind died. This is what it means to be up the creek without a paddle, a proverb he only then fully understood. Drifting with the current down river, he desperately wished for wind. It came just before he reached the Tappan Zee Bridge, and it came blustery cold straight out of the north. Wet and shivering, he recognized the need for one more indispensable item: a foul weather suit. Two, if Roswita some day actually would go sailing with him.

Chapter Sixteen

In May of 1965, Mrs. Dubois secured a contract with Bloomingdale's for Roswita, whose pictures now graced the pages of that retailer's catalogues, from cosmetics and lingerie to jewelry, handbags and accessories. Well on her way to becoming a successful photo model, she quit her receptionist job at Max Factor.

When AID took over a medium-sized automotive parts firm that produced components for GMC trucks, Walter advanced to general manager, a promotion that secured his position in the company. His professional performance, his capability and company minded conduct had earned him the respect of coworkers and superiors. Money problems no longer were their first concern, although Roswita had no secure income since she gave up her steady job.

The old Mercury, their dream car, was ready for the junkyard and Walter bought an almost new Honda Accord hatchback.

"We also need another boat, a bigger one," said Roswita. "You know that. I'm not getting back in that boat, after what happened. ROXY is just too small. You know that, Walter."

She referred to the incident on a sweltering August afternoon. They had been caught in a thunderstorm when a gust capsized their boat. Floatation devices kept it from sinking, but they failed to right it; the wind was too strong, the waves too choppy. Walter and Roswita, hanging onto the boat, drifted to the rocky shore of Croton Park, just south of Sing Sing, the infamous prison. A park ranger, who found them scrambling out of the water, took them into custody and phoned the prison to find out if someone had recently escaped. After two hours he released the two shipwreck survivors. They bailed out the boat and sailed back across the river to Nyack.

Roswita had become a proficient shipmate in the two years they sailed on the Hudson in their tiny sloop *ROXY*, but since the ordeal of that Sunday in August she refused to go sailing again. "A little bigger, Walter. We can afford it. Mrs. Dubois is trying to get me a TV commercial. Real money, Walter. Real money."

She also insisted on switching to a more prestigious marina. "How can we invite anybody to Koenig's crummy place, once we have a bigger boat? A marina you call that? Please…! It's a dump!" She was right, of course, and he began looking around for a bigger, more stable, more comfortable boat. Then, he promised, they would find another marina.

It is no secret, in fact a well-known, yet unexplained phenomenon, that some women more than others exude manifestations of availability. Roswita had such a quality. "Men pick up on such signs, much like dogs trained in sniffing out explosives or drugs," she said.

The incident with Renaldo, more than two years ago, was not her only escapade. There were the president of a Madison Avenue advertising agency, with whom she had an affair lasting several weeks, a VP of a fashion magazine, the buyer of a clothing line at Bloomingdale's, and others. All were married, but that did not stop them—or her. Walter knew of her ramblings; she was not secretive about them.

"It's all meaningless, Walter. You know that," she assured him, and it did not bother him—well, it did a little.

"But why, Roswita?" he had asked her once or twice, out of curiosity, not to reproach her.

"I don't know. It's in my nature, I guess," she answered lightheartedly. "You knew that from the start. You found it intriguing, you said." And snuggling up to him, "some men find me irresistible. Like you. I like that. And they are all different. I like that too."

They lived together, but they often went their separate ways—well, she did. Walter was monogamous, partly because he did not have the opportunities she had. Aside from AID's strict views on relationships within the company, there were no female employees that raised his pulse or caused a stirring in his loin. He would have loved a fling with some of Roswita's friends, Felicia Napolitano, for example, but she was lesbian, or Helen Rossi, that beauty with blue-black hair and a dazzling smile who, according to Roswita, was about to marry her boyfriend.

Roswita never brought home any of her male acquaintances, with whom she entertained intimate relationships; her ethics did not allow that. "Those things don't belong here," she emphasized, but she asked friends over, both men and women, for drinks and games, and sometimes such gatherings ran a little out of control.

They also were invited to parties and once, at the mansion of a TV producer in the Hamptons, someone suggested playing Keys in the Hat. The hour was late, all were more or less drunk. House keys and car keys were collected in a hat which then was passed around. Everyone picked a key or a set of keys out of the hat and thus was determined who would be partners for the rest of the night. Most of the ten or twelve participants were happy with the outcome—there were only attractive people in their twenties, thirties and forties, and most were somehow connected with the fashion or entertainment business.

They came together for a catered brunch on the veranda overlooking the ocean, to clear away their hangovers, and perhaps the memories of the night. Roswita came out with a bearded man in his forties. She saw immediately that Walter has had a good time. Freshly showered and shaved, he looked handsome in his gray slacks and blue blazer. Beside him sat the young brunette, a Broadway starlet, with whom he had spent the night.

"That was fun," said Roswita on their drive home, "although I've not had such a great time. But you really got lucky. Who was that?"

"I have no idea, don't recall her name. Why didn't you have a great time?"

"Ah, it was okay. I had met him before. Greg. He writes not very good screenplays. He cries when he's finished. I don't like unhappy people."

"He cries?"

"Yeah. Misses his wife, I guess. Just got divorced. I'm not gonna see him again. Are you seeing What's-her-name again?"

"No. I don't think so. I don't know anything about her, except that she had a part in… forgot what play."

"I am glad you had your spree. That's what I like about us, we don't judge."

"I don't intend to make it a habit, though."

"Want to stop at Felicia's? See if she's home?" she teased him. "Take the next exit."

Walter drove straight home after that night at the TV producer's mansion on Long Island. He had to prepare himself for a meeting the following Monday in Detroit, for which he had to take an early flight. The same day Roswita had a meeting with Mrs. Dubois and the young production manager from an ad agency.

"It is not a very glamorous project, Roswita," Mrs. Dubois told her. "I agree, but it is a start. I urge you to accept it, and if it actually produces sales, others will follow." She nodded toward the young man. "Isn't that right, Mr. O'Neil?"

Roswita was reluctant. "Bathroom cleaner? Scrubbing a toilet?"

"You're not scrubbing a toilet," said O'Neil. "You just spray the tile with the product, say a few words and then the logo flashes over the screen. We will have you in a short bathrobe, you bend down, maybe show a little flesh... We'll work something out with the film crew. The budget allows for no more than a twenty-five second ad. You may appear for just ten, fifteen seconds." He looked at his watch. "I have to hurry back," and to Mrs. Dubois, "I'll give you a call tomorrow. Miss Peschel has the job, if she wants it." He got up, shook hands with Mrs. Dubois, smiled at Roswita, and left.

"Twelve hundred dollars, Roswita. Think about it. Twelve hundred dollars for fifteen seconds."

"I'll call you. I have to think it over." She left Mrs. Dubois's office and took a cab home. Twelve hundred dollars, went through her head. Fifteen seconds work. It's not gonna be fifteen seconds. It's gonna be a whole day. But twelve hundred dollars...

Mrs. Dubois phoned her late afternoon, asking for an answer. "I'll call you tomorrow morning," Roswita told her. Sure, she makes a bundle on the deal, for very little work.

When Walter came home after midnight, he found her in bed, but awake; she had not been able to fall sleep. "Oh, you are awake? Couldn't sleep, huh?"

"How was your flight? Tired? Want a drink?"

"No, I had a couple on the flight. You?"

"If you have one with me. Listen, if they offered you twelve hundred dollars for fifteen seconds on TV, would you do it?"

"Depends. What would I have to do?"

"Not you. I had this meeting today with Mrs. Dubois and a guy from an advertising agency, and..."

"Oh yeah, how did that go?"

"Well, they want me to do a TV ad. Bathroom cleaner. I don't know. Will that hurt my reputation? You know, bathroom tile, toilet..."

"Roswita, you don't have a reputation. Not yet, anyway. Did you say twelve hundred dollars? You never had an offer like that."

"I know. So, you think I should take it?"

"I think you should." He prepared two drinks in the kitchen and called back to her, "By the way, how would you think about moving to Detroit?"

"What? Detroit? Where is that? Are you out of your mind? No way!"

"That's what I told them."

In the morning Roswita phoned Mrs. Dubois. "You can tell them I accept, but only if I don't have to clean a toilet. Please, make that clear to them."

As she had expected, the shoot went on for five hours, doing the same thing over and over again. Then O'Neil asked her to have a drink with him, but she declined and went home. She called Walter at his office. "I am exhausted. Let's just order a pizza for tonight and maybe a bottle of wine."

"Why don't we go out to eat somewhere?"

"Walter, I am soaking in the tub. I want to stay in and relax. It was grueling. Grueling, I say."

Through the winter months, Roswita sprayed grimy bathroom tiles and tubs with *StarBrite Bath&Tile Mist*. On TV, that is. In a commercial, interrupting the morning shows and afternoon soap operas, she is first seen only from the back, wrapped in a towel, with bare shoulders and legs, humming a happy tune. Then she turns to face the camera and says, *It's easy with StarBrite Bath&Tile Mist. Just spray and rinse.* Then the aerosol container flashes on the screen; underneath, *Use only as directed.* She comes back, smiling beautifully, showing the can. *StarBrite Bath&Tile Mist*, she announces joyfully. *You will never use anything else.* Her towel slips to reveal the top of her breasts. *Ooops*, she laughs—and it's over.

Roswita did not like to watch television in the daytime. She saw her commercial once. Me on TV, she thought. Pretty good, and funny at the end. Twelve hundred bucks, that's not too much. It's not even enough.

"Did you see it, Walter? Did you like it?"

"Yes, I did. And so did a lot of people at the office. They had not seen you for so long, but recognized you right away. Your hair, and that accent."

"Walter, you once mentioned Detroit. You weren't serious, right? I would never want to move out of New York."

"No. They just brought it up briefly at that meeting, that it wouldn't be such a bad idea. But they knew I didn't consider it."

"My career is in New York. I will have more work. They already told me. There is no place like New York. Let's not ever move."

"No. But we should think about another apartment, a condo or a house."

Walter's position in the company was established, his income supplemented with bonuses and profit sharing. He wore expensive designer suits, shirts and ties. Roswita had a natural flair for fashion and Walter loved to see her in the latest styles. Elegant or casual, she always looked sexy, never trashy.

"I love this apartment, but I see the need for more room. The closet is crammed, our clothes can't breathe and get wrinkled. Where could we go? I will not move out of Manhattan. Maybe Brooklyn, but that's it. No Queens, or the Bronx. Staten Island…" She mimicked gagging. "But where, Walter, where?"

"I will look into it."

"And, Walter, have you forgotten about the boat? You haven't been out on the water for a long time. Don't you think we should have a nice sailboat? People with money like us have boats, you know."

"I haven't forgotten, Roswita, but one thing at a time. We can't just…"

"I know, I know. I'm sorry. I didn't mean to…"

"It's okay."

Walter had been quietly searching for a larger sailboat since the previous summer and in the spring of 1968, he decided on a two-year old 36-foot Cape Dory. The boat showed up at the Nyack Yacht Club, with a *For Sale* sign on the bow pulpit. It was one of those forced divorce sales. Walter put a bid on it and won for the ridiculously low price of forty-eight thousand dollars.

Roswita was thrilled when she saw it out there at anchor in front of the Yacht Club. "Well, now that is a boat! How do we get out there?"

"She comes with a dinghy and outboard motor. It's right here."

They went out to the Cape Dory. "*FOXY LADY*—what kind of a name is that?" Roswita asked as they came close to the boat. "Must we keep it?"

"We will register her as *ROXY II*." They climbed on board.

"I want to see inside."

"Below decks, Roswita. You need to sharpen your nautical lingo." Walter opened the companionway and they went below.

"She is beautiful!" Roswita admired the upholstery and the mahogany woodwork. She inspected the main cabin, the bathroom, the forward cabin, the kitchen.

"On a boat you must use the nautical terms: the saloon, the head, the fo'c'sle and the galley. And this is the quarter berth, our sleeping quarters."

"I have to learn all that; but, Walter, we can invite people, have cocktails on board, sleep-overs, play Keys in the Hat…"

"Roswita, the boat is for sailing, primarily."

"Oh, I know. I'm just kidding."

On a windy day in early May, they sailed *ROXY II* down the Hudson to the Barren Island Marina near Sheepshead Bay in Brooklyn, Walter at the helm and Roswita huddled in the cockpit in her new foul weather suit.

"It's some sixteen years since I sailed a boat this size, Roswita. I was twenty-one then. Around Denmark, a gung-ho crew of young guys. What a cruise that was! I told you about it."

"Yeah, I know. You got into a fight somewhere." After awhile, they had just passed the George Washington Bridge, "Walter, when will we get there?"

"I don't know, another six or seven hours. Why?"

That was the beginning of a new era. Their lives became caught up in a tailspin, a vortex, a descent into excesses they did not know how to control.

PART IV
But why, Roswita?

Chapter Seventeen

Walter had not been in touch with his parents on a regular basis. He had limited his correspondence to a card for Christmas, his mother's birthday or some such occasions, supplemented now and then with a phone call. He grew up with little attention from his father, and when he went to Frankfurt at age twenty to learn the fur trade, he did so on his father's insistence, but rarely received any money from him to add to his meager apprentice wages. During his two years in Vienna, he never heard from him.

He came to America without consulting his parents and without their approval. Shortly after his arrival in New York, Walter informed his mother that he had abandoned the fur trade and that he had found employment in the automotive industry. His father was furious that his son broke the three hundred year-old family tradition of furriers and fur merchants. Since then, they had not spoken another word.

Walter never included his father in the greetings he sent or asked about him when he made his rare phone calls and his mother never mentioned him, until the day she informed him that his father had died. "Won't you come to his funeral?" she pleaded. "He asked for you as he lay dying."

"He never asked for me before," Walter said to Roswita. "What should I do? Should I now fly over there to bury him?"

"Do you want to?"

"No."

"Then don't. Walter, I have to leave. I promised Helen."

"Roswita, wait. You never talk about your parents. What were they like?"

"I hardly knew my father. He died in the war. Then my mother was always running around—other men, you know. I was raised by my aunt, my father's sister. She lived across the street."

"In Leipzig?"

"Yes, in Leipzig. Walter, I really have to go."

Other men—always running around. So, that's where she's got it, from her mother. Always running around…

On Monday morning, the day after his mother's phone call, he concluded he would not fly across the ocean to bury the man who had despised him. He did feel sorry for his mother, but she had family, a younger brother as well as cousins and nephews.

The take-over of a major auto parts discount chain had propelled Walter yet another step up the corporate ladder. As vice president for customer relations and product safety, Walter filled one of the most demanding positions at AID. From his new office at company headquarters in the Chrysler Building, he had a spectacular view over midtown Manhattan.

He could see the Seventy-ninth Street high-rise, where he and Roswita had recently bought an apartment.

Walking distance, he reflected briefly, yet worlds apart. Roswita drew him into a lifestyle he had so far experienced more or less as a bystander, an outsider. In his youth, in Frankfurt, he saw himself sometimes as a bohemian, although he had remained on the sidelines, participating in free-spirited pleasures. He swam along with the stream, but never too far from the shore to catch a branch on which to pull himself to safety. Now, in New York, he was swept along in midstream, but he could not allow his personal life to interfere with his professional one, and he directed his mental resources back to his work that required his full attention.

Their circle of friends, more aptly called a carousing crowd, consisted solely of Roswita's acquaintances. Walter's only friends—and again that is an inaccurate description—were Gerda and Joe Chang. He had not seen them for years; his courtesy calls grew further and further apart. Straitlaced as they were, they would not fit into an environment of unrestrained indulgences.

Walter lived two lives: one as an executive in the corporate world, the other of limitless excesses, Roswita's world. Agencies on Madison Avenue considered her valuable property. She now had continuous work, which brought with it endless partying. Walter, an attractive bachelor of considerable stature, was a regular among the Broadway and Madison Avenue thrill seekers. Not being married, both were fair game, not that it would have mattered.

"I have a surprise for you, Walter, if you play your cards right," Roswita announced as they drove out of the city in their new Mercedes to Westchester. "You'll know some of the people there." She paused to test his level of interest.

"A surprise? What kind of a surprise? You know I don't like surprises."

"This one you'll like."

"Donald Trump? Is he going to be there?"

"No, I don't think so. I asked Helen Rossi to come."

"Helen? You told me I have no chance."

"I'll seduce her fiancé. I know I can."

"Her fiancé? They still didn't get married?"

"He once tried to get me in the sack. I told her about it and they broke up. Now they're back together, but it's not gonna work, she told me. She wants out."

"Who is he? I don't want any trouble."

"Roger something or other. He pronounces it Rogé. Works at Lincoln Center. Lighting, I think. You'll meet him tonight."

They arrived late at the stately villa of a real estate investor. An attendant in a short black dress and white apron ushered Roswita and Walter in. The party was in full swing, a gathering of beautiful people and those with money, sitting or standing in groups, glasses in hand, talking, joking, laughing. There was a hint of marijuana in the air; in one corner a threesome was snorting cocaine.

Few noticed the new arrivals or paid any attention, others waved hello. Walter spotted Helen, her shiny black hair half a head above the crowd. "The guy with the long hair, is that Roger?"

"Yes," said Roswita. "Let's walk over there."

"Hi, Roxy. Walter, meet Rogé," Helen greeted them.

Walter couldn't shake his hand; Roger had a glass in one hand and a joint in the other.

"Hey, man. How you doin'? Roswita, want a drag?" He held the joint out for her to take a puff.

"Roswita," Walter said half-loud close to her ear. "Remember? We're staying away from that stuff." They had pledged to each other not ever to use drugs.

"Oh, yeah," and she pushed Roger's hand with the joint toward Helen who inhaled deeply.

Walter and Roswita mingled, picked up an hors d'oeuvre and a glass of something that was passed around, but soon found themselves back in a group with Roger and Helen, who was already quite tipsy.

"Walter, when will I finally get to see your boat? Roxy says it's big and beautiful. Rogé knows how to sail, don't you Rogé?" She shot a challenging look at Roger, mocking him.

"Sure," Roger asserted.

"I have yet to see him handle a sailboat. We went out once with Stephan, but he didn't let him do anything."

"Let's go right now, Walter. What do you say? This party stinks. You're not too drunk to drive, are you? We'll just sneak out."

"Donald Trump might show up. I've never met him," Walter objected.

'It's the middle of the night. He's not coming. Come on. Let's go."

Helen walked over to the couple with whom they had come, talked briefly, and then the four of them left.

Roswita arranged for Helen to sit in the front with Walter. As soon as Roger and Roswita had taken their seats in the back, he lit another joint, passed it to Roswita, but she refused. They drove south on the Taconic Parkway and before they reached the Henry Hudson Parkway, Walter could no longer see them in the rearview mirror.

Helen looked back over her shoulder. "They're already going at it," she said to Walter, giggled and put one hand in his lap.

They arrived at the marina past midnight. The air was mild, the boat yard and the docks eerie in the sparse illumination. "Shoes off," said Walter, "unless you wear topsiders." They stepped on board *ROXY II* and he turned on the lights below.

"Wow," escaped Helen. Roger looked around as if to say, No big deal, I've seen it all before. Walter opened a bottle of scotch. Roswita showed Helen around, using all the correct nautical terms. Walter did not like anyone smoking in the cabin, but said nothing when Roger lit yet another joint.

They drank their scotch and talked about the people at the party. Roger was incoherent and busy trying to unzip Roswita's skirt. Helen spilt her drink in Walter's lap and tried to suck the liquor from his pants, giggling, "Oh, this is fun!"

"I take the forward cabin," said Roswita, nudging Roger to get up. "Come on, and no more smoking, or you're no good for anything."

Walter stood in the galley making coffee and scrambling eggs. Bacon sizzled in the frying pan. Helen did not stir; she was severely hung over. "You'd better get out of there and into the fresh air," he tried to coax her back to life. "I'll make you a Bloody Mary. We can all use one." He heard noise coming from the fo'c'sle.

Roger came out of the head. "Roswita is still sleeping," he said instead of Good morning. "Do I smell bacon?"

"Rogé, is that you?" Helen's weak voice from the quarter berth. "I am sick. That smell... I want to throw up."

He didn't respond, didn't seem to care. "I feel great. Are we going out today?" he asked Walter. "How's the weather?"

"No. I have to go to the office later. Maybe some other time." He served the eggs. "Go, get Roswita. I'll take care of Helen."

Later they sat at the table, each with a glass of Bloody Mary. Helen shuddered, but she revived as soon as the alcohol entered her bloodstream. "A shot of vodka always does the trick," said Walter. "I learned that a long time ago."

"And you taught me," said Roswita joining them. "Almost every morning I have some vodka, straight from the bottle. It works wonders. I have to have a clear head and look my best, you know, when I work. Helen, you too..."

"I don't drink the way you do, Roxy. I don't know how you can keep it up. The day you show up drunk for a shoot, or with bloodshot eyes, believe me... They'll throw you out. I told you that."

"That's why I have a shot in the morning. Anyway, Walter, you're okay? You had a good time, huh? You wanted it for so long," she whispered in his ear, then turned to Helen. "How was it? You know, Walter is great in bed. Or were you too drunk?"

"Is there some more of the eggs and bacon?" Roger asked. "I'll have another cup of coffee, if there is some."

"Help yourself," said Walter.

"Are you embarrassed?" Roswita asked Roger. "You don't want to talk about it, huh?" To Helen she said, "He was stoned. Is he any better when he's not stoned?"

"Enough of this talk," Roger reacted angrily. "If we're not going sailing, we might as well leave."

"Rogé, don't be so rude. We leave when we're all ready," Helen chided him.

"I think, Helen is right. Your drinking, partying and screwing around will catch up with you, eventually. Think about it, Roswita." He was also concerned about his position in the company. "We can't let our private lives interfere with our professional ones."

They had dropped Roger and Helen off at her Westside apartment. Walter parked the Mercedes in the basement garage of their Seventy-ninth Street luxury building. "You really have to go to your office?" Roswita asked him in the elevator.

"No, I just said it. That Roger, or Rogé, he's getting on my nerves. You don't like him very much either, huh? Last night, did he, did you... I mean, if he was so stoned, could he..."

"He was okay. Second time he fell asleep before he finished. I was doing all right. Twice."

They entered their apartment. "Let's take a shower, then I want to sleep an hour or so." He undressed while Roswita poured herself a drink. "Roswita, we really have to think about this. I neglect most of my social obligations with, you know, the president and others, and their wives. That doesn't look good. Next Friday is the opening of the New

Jersey Distribution Center. I think we should go. There'll be a cocktail party afterwards. All the big shots and their wives."

She went into the shower with him. "But that's when we go on vacation."

"Do my back. We leave Saturday morning. Flight's at nine fifteen."

"You will meet O'Neil, from Schuster & O'Neil."

"Who's O'Neil?" He stepped out of the shower and put on his bathrobe. "Do I know him? Schuster & O'Neil, the ad people?"

"Pat O'Neil. The one who gave me my first TV spot. You know, the one with the bathroom cleaner—what was it called? Remember? Starshine something."

He slumped down on their bed. "Starbrite."

"Yeah, right." Wrapped in a towel she stretched out beside him. "So, he's flying out with us. He made it big last year, when he joined Schuster."

"Did you... With him?"

"No. I wasn't interested then. Now? I don't know. He's young. Younger than me. Only thirty-six or seven, I guess."

"Married?"

"I don't think so."

Walter drove back to the marina to clean up *ROXY II* after the night of debauchery. He came home to find a note pinned to the hook where he hung his jacket. *Helen called. I'll be at her place tonight. She needs me. Call you later. Ros.*

He crumbled the note as the phone rang. "Helen has a black eye. He hit her. She was able to call the police, but he was gone when they came."

"What if he comes back?"

"That's why she wants me here. She made a report."

"What if he beats you up, too?"

"Then he gets a black eye, and a bloody nose to boot. I don't take shit like that. Helen will be out of work for a week, at least."

"Be careful. Want me to come over there?"

"No, no. Then there'd be trouble if he shows up. That's what the fight was about. You and her. He hates you, thinks because of your money, you know…"

"Call me if there's trouble. Or call the police." He hung up. I really cannot get involved in this. My name in a police report… No no, I have to stay out of this.

He did not hear from Roswita until Monday afternoon, when she called him at the office. "He didn't come back. I am still with her. She will file for a restraining order tomorrow. I'm going home now. See you tonight."

On Friday they drove to Jersey City for the ribbon cutting of the new AID Distribution Center. "I will introduce you as my wife."

"But, Walter, don't they know me?"

"The president and the other VPs are all Germans from the parent company in Stuttgart. They rotate every two to four years. Nobody knows you. The mayor will be there, maybe even the governor. It's a big deal for New Jersey. Helps the state with the unemployment. There will be champagne. Just two, Roswita, please."

"I'll be on my best behavior. I promise."

As all such occasions, it was a boring event, with boring speeches, boring small talk afterwards and cheap champagne. Walter had vaguely prepared a short speech, in case he would be called upon, but that did not happen and, still early in the afternoon, they were on their way back through the Holland Tunnel into Manhattan.

The car back in the garage, they went for a quick salad in a bistro on First Avenue, and then they packed their bags for the flight from La Guardia to St. Thomas.

"Are you taking a suit, or just casual wear? I'll be in a bikini most of the time. We'll go directly on the boat."

"I'll bring one pair of white pants. The rest, shorts and T-shirts. Pack one gown, the thin flowery one. Now, who exactly are we meeting there? Who made all the arrangements?"

"You know Gustav Melchior and his wife Vicky from last week's party. She used to be a dancer. "

"Know them? Hardly. You just pointed them out to me. Then we went over to Roger and Helen."

"Well, he and Ben Gould are friends for years. Ben, you know... well, I told you about him and me. Much of my work I have because of him. He's really big on Madison Avenue."

"Yeah, you once slept with him. When was that? A couple of years ago?"

"Not just once, Walter. He's very important. He is married, but she never shows up with him. She's a drunk. From one rehab to the next."

"So, Gustav Melchior and Ben Gould. Who else?"

"Pat O'Neil. He'll bring someone. We'll meet them on the plane."

Chapter Eighteen

They met at the gate for the flight to San Juan. Pat O'Neil introduced a skinny blonde as Katja from the Ukraine. Walter and Pat, who met for the first time, shook hands.

"Gustav Melchior comes in on his jet together with Ben Gould and their wives. We will meet them at the Yacht Haven in St. Thomas," Pat told them.

In San Juan they boarded a small plane for the short hop to Charlotte Amalie. A taxi delivered them to the Yacht Haven. Roswita and Katja from the Ukraine went to sit under an umbrella near the pool, and ordered piña coladas. Out on the dock, next to the harbormaster's office, was a sign *Island Charters*, where a porter set down their bags. Walter and Pat asked for someone in charge of the *SEA WITCH*.

"Looking for me?" A young man in white shorts came toward them. Imprinted on his blue T-shirt was a sailboat above the name *SEA WITCH*. "Hi. I am Karl. You are with Mr. Melchior's party? They'll arrive tonight. Britt, my mate, will take care of you in just a little bit. She's still busy with the provisioning." He pointed to their luggage. "Leave this right here. You go and make yourselves comfortable by the pool. Order any drinks; they're on us."

Roswita and Katja from the Ukraine were on their third piña colada, the men had their second beer, when a young girl in white shorts and blue shirt came to show them to the boat.

"Hello, I am Britt, the mate on the SEA WITCH. You can come on board now. If you will follow me. Your gear is already on board. If there is anything you want, anything at all, just call me."

The seventy-six foot yacht was docked at the head of the pier. Karl welcomed them on board. "Mr. and Mrs. Melchior have the aft cabin, Mr. and Mrs. Gould will be in the stateroom on the port side. The main cabin accommodates you," he addressed both Walter and Pat. "When you are ready to retire, Britt converts it into comfortable sleeping quarters."

Roswita asked Pat, "You really think Ben Gould brings his wife, that lush?"

"I think so. I have never met her. I heard she was a prostitute in Holland. She's Dutch, you know. Her name is Beatrix."

"A dancer and a prostitute?" Walter was amused. "How old is the dancer?"

"Vicky? I guess they're both in their late forties or so, Gustav and Vicky. Ben and Beatrix, too."

"And don't forget Katja from the Ukraine," Roswita laughed.

"What?" asked Katja. "But I am only twenty-two."

Roswita gave her skeletal frame a hug. "We are going to have so much fun."

The Melchiors and entourage arrived as the sky turned opaque. Darkness comes quickly in these tropical latitudes. A porter deposited their baggage on the dock. Karl and Britt carried it on board. Vicky made a few dance steps, which wasn't too impressive; her body was no longer that of a dancer. Jovial Gustav prevented her from making a fool of herself. "Now now, Vicky, careful here on the dock." Ben aided Beatrix as she gingerly stepped on the deck of the *SEA WITCH*.

Walter and Roswita, Pat and Katja from the Ukraine were in the cockpit. The two men stood to greet the new arrivals, first Gustav Melchior, whom they considered their host, then Ben Gould. They bowed to their wives.

"Good, good." Gustav had a strong voice. "And who are the two lovely young ladies? Ah, yes, yes. Roswita. Charming, charming."

"May I present Katja? She is from the Ukraine," Pat hastened to explain.

"Katja from the Ukraine. Very nice, very nice."

Roswita talked to Ben Gould. "You haven't met Walter? This is Walter Hansen, my fiancé." She didn't mean to say fiancé; it just slipped out. "I am sure I have mentioned him."

"Of course. I'll call you Walter, you call me Ben. Let's drop the formalities."

"I'd like that," said Walter as they shook hands.

Britt interrupted the introductions. "May I suggest a welcoming drink?"

"Yes, yes. And something to eat. Where is Karl, our skipper? Ah, there you are, there you are. What have you prepared for us? Do we have champagne on this vessel?"

"Right away, sir," Britt answered for Karl. "We have a smorgasbord. May I serve it here in the cockpit? And, of course, champagne."

The cockpit was large enough for the four couples to sit, and the extended table had room for the platters laden with smoked fish, cold cuts, cheeses and fresh bread. Britt served the champagne.

Ben spoke calmly to Beatrix; his hand gestures were unmistakable to which she answered, "Oh, just a little sip."

They feasted on the delicacies and the conversation was animated.

"Where does one sleep here? I already miss my bed." Beatrix had more than just a sip. "Oh god, I miss my bed."

Britt was always present when needed. "Ma'am, your stateroom is ready, if you wish to retire."

Ben helped his wife down the companionway to their accommodations.

Tiny, ninety-pound Katja from the Ukraine had handled all that drinking well, but the moment she assumed a horizontal position, she passed out. Pat tried but failed to get a response from her. He gave up, and both slept solidly into the morning.

Voices coming from the adjacent stateroom kept Walter and Roswita awake. "I don't want you to sleep with her," they heard Beatrix whining. "I am never enough for you."

"Go to sleep. You're drunk," Ben shouted. "And don't you dare talk about her. You'd better remember where you came from."

"I hate you."

"Go ahead. I hate you, too."

"You hear that, Roswita? They're talking about you," Walter whispered.

"I know. What is she complaining about? She must have slept with hundreds. Now, all of a sudden, she is jealous? Come on, cuddle me." Then they fell asleep.

Preparations for getting underway roused the sleepers as dawn crept over the eastern horizon. Karl greeted them, "It's eight to ten hours to Virgin Gorda. Wind's twenty knots straight out of the east. Beautiful. It will be a little rough, though."

Beatrix was antagonistic toward Roswita during the entire passage along the south shores of St. Thomas and St. John and tacking through Sir Frances Drake Channel. She annoyed everyone, including the crew, with sly remarks and innuendos about 'that slut' and what her husband 'that wimp' sees in her. Walter restrained Roswita from responding and, when no one paid attention, Beatrix resorted to accusing Karl for sailing recklessly. "Does he even know what he's doing?"

"Leave him alone. He's doing a fine job," her husband reprimanded her.

"And where is Britt? Nowhere to be seen when one needs a drink. Ah, there you are. Bring me a vodka martini, dear."

"Ma'am, I really would not... I mean in these rough sea conditions."

"Bring her the goddamn drink, please, Britt," said Ben. "Maybe that will shut her up."

In the evening, docked at the marina in Spanish Harbour, they had dinner at the restaurant on the premises. The bickering between Ben and Beatrix went on and no one seemed to notice that Pat and Roswita had left the table before the dessert was served.

Walter slid over to the chair next to Katja from the Ukraine. "Did you see them leave? Did Pat say something?"

"No, he didn't have to say anything. I may be young, but I'm not dumb. When we all were in the cockpit, where were they? Below, making out."

"And you don't mind?"

"Pat and I, we're not a couple. Just casual, you know. I work for him and, you know, sometimes... Well, sometimes we do stuff."

"You want to go somewhere? Look around the island, and then go back to the boat?"

"Let's have another drink first. I like to be a little tipsy. And then, sure."

Little five-foot Katja from the Ukraine was delightfully tipsy as they walked along a dirt road. Her boyish hair was cut so short, it didn't move in the warm night breeze. Walter ruffled it with his hand and she snickered playfully. They stopped and kissed.

"Why go to the boat? Let's do it right here in the dunes," she said blatantly and pulled him toward the overgrown beach.

Taken aback for a second, Walter held her at arm's length. "Huh. Are all Ukrainians so brazenly outspoken?"

"We say what we mean."

"We? You?"

"Ukrainians, Russians, Poles. We are Slavs—we say what we mean. Come on, or you want to talk? You Americans are all talk and never say what you mean."

After what must have been more than an hour, they went back to the dock. As they passed the restaurant, Ben called them over. "Walter, where is Roswita? I wanted to talk to her. Did she leave with Pat O'Neil?"

"Talk? You want to talk? I don't know where she is. Ben, that's your wife sitting right next to you."

"Yeah, so? She's drunk."

"I don't care anymore," Beatrix slurred and let her chin drop to her bony chest.

Walter and Katja walked out to the dock. "Let us sit in the cockpit for awhile," he said. "They might be, you know…"

"Having sex, you mean. Don't you want to join them?"

Oh, this girl is something else. Who would have thought? Tiny Katja from the Ukraine. "Let's stay here."

A short time later Ben Gould came on board, practically carrying his wife. "I'll just put her to bed. Then I want to talk to you," he said pointedly and somewhat forceful to Walter. "Preferably before Gustav and Vicky come back."

Walter did not like his tone. "What do you want to talk about?"

When Ben came out again, Katja went below. "What I wanted to talk to you about… You obviously don't care much about Roswita. So, I think you wouldn't mind if I, you know, took a little care of her. Know what I mean?"

"Ah, wouldn't that be up to her? And, whether I care for her, or we care for each other, that's really none of your business."

"Now now, you don't have to get so…"

Gustav and Vicky interrupted him as they came on board. "Nice dinner, nice dinner," Gustav boomed. "Is Beatrix all right?"

"All taken care of," Ben answered. To Walter he said, "So, we understand each other."

"Perfectly."

"Good. I'm going to bed now."

"So are we, so are we. Careful, Vicky, careful on the steps."

Walter was left alone in the cockpit.

Roswita came up the companionway. "Beautiful night, isn't it, Walter?"

"Yes, it is."

At noontime the following day, the *SEA WITCH* anchored in the harbor of Roadtown among dozens of sailboats and powerboats of all sizes and many nationalities. Britt had prepared a bouillabaisse and set the table in the cockpit. She brought out a large tureen with the steaming stew of seafood.

"What's bouilla-what-ever?" querulous Beatrix was skeptical. "What's in it?"

Ben said, "It's fish. You'll like it. Or else you can go and eat ashore—alone."

She said no more.

"There are two kinds of fish, scallops, shrimp and bits of lobster tails with potatoes, onion and tomatoes," Britt explained. "All simmered together in clam broth. My specialty," she added proudly. "I recommend beer with it. We have Heineken."

Gustav applauded, Beatrix made a face and the rest of them voiced their approval.

In the afternoon, they sailed for Jost Van Dyke. Walter asked Roswita to sit with him on the foredeck. "Did Ben Gould talk to you?"

"He wanted to know why I avoided him and went off with Pat."

"What did you say?"

"I told him, that's how I am. I do stuff like that. 'Besides,' I told him, 'you have your wife here,' and he said, 'you know how it is with her—always drunk.'"

"Must be tough for him."

"I don't know why he doesn't throw her overboard. Drunk, you know. She could stumble and... Who would know the difference?"

"Did he ask you about me?"

"Sure. Why you didn't care, he wanted to know. I said, we had an agreement. Walter, I will have to sleep with him. He is my bread and butter, you know. I can't lose him. He can make it difficult for me. I would never get another job. That's how this business is. He is that important."

"Oh boy. That can get ugly. Why did you have to do it with Pat? Why, Roswita?"

"Oh come on, Walter. You know me. But I also did it for you, so you could have Katja from the Ukraine. How was it, by the way?"

"That Katja, she's really something. You wouldn't believe it."

The anchor went down in Great Harbour of Jost Van Dyke. Walter and Roswita went back into the cockpit. There was an altercation between Ben and Pat. Beatrix couldn't contain herself. "Oh, here she comes, the whore you are fighting over."

"Look who is talking. Why don't you shut your mouth," Roswita threw at her.

Gustav appeased them in his patriarchal voice. "Now now, we don't want to go on like this, do we? In this beautiful harbor? Let's all go ashore and have a good time. What do you say, Vicky? What do you say, huh? Karl—where is he? Ah,

Karl, rig the dinghy and take us ashore. Don't we all want to go ashore?"

Karl and Britt launched the Zodiac. They all piled into the dinghy and Karl ferried them to the beach.

Roswita was the last to disembark. "I forgot something," she said. "Karl, please take me back to the boat."

Ben Gould recognized his cue. He climbed back into the dinghy and returned to the SEA WITCH with Roswita.

Karl had one of the finest jobs on earth. Sailing was his passion, and making money at the same time, what could be better? But, as in everything, there was a downside to it.

He and Britt were having a nightcap in the cockpit." I am doing this for a couple of years now," he said, "but this is the weirdest bunch of people I ever sailed around these islands with. Now I have to wait until they call to be picked up."

"Want me to go in and pick 'em up?

"No, I better do that. They'll be stone drunk. They'll need help. I don't want anybody to fall and drown or something. Why don't you go to bed. Those two down there won't need you anymore."

Ben and Roswita had had the main cabin to themselves, but after midnight Ben went to sleep in his stateroom. "Then they don't find us together. Thanks, Roswita. I so enjoy being with you."

In the early morning hours, Gustav called on the walkie-talkie. "Will you, please, do us the favor." Karl went in to pick them up. All had consumed substantial amounts of liquor. Gustav and Vicky had their hands full keeping Beatrix on an even keel.

Karl told Britt, "O'Neil and Hansen had a fight at Foxy's Bar. Mr. Melchior told me. Yesterday it was Ben Gould and O'Neil, fighting over Roswita, that sexy blonde. And Gould's wife, the drunk, fans the fire."

"I thought Roswita was Walter Hansen's wife."

"Not according to their passports. She is Roswita Peschel. And the other blonde, the one with the Russian name, she came with O'Neil. I don't know their status. They are all mixed up. Mr. Melchior tries to keep the peace. He and his wife are the only ones with a sense of normalcy, but this is like sitting on a volcano, waiting for it to erupt."

"What are your options, as the skipper?"

"I can cut the trip short, if I think it necessary for safety. That's in my contract with Island Charters. But at this point I don't see enough of a reason for it.

"Three more days," said Britt.

The *SEA WITCH* remained at anchor in Great Harbour until noon. Relative order was restored, hangovers cured, tensions relieved. On leaving Jost Van Dyke for St. John, Pat O'Neil asked Karl if there were a good spot to do some snorkeling before sailing into Cruz Bay.

"Christmas Cove. Anyone else would like to stop at Christmas Cove? We can spend a couple of hours there and still get into Cruz Bay before nightfall."

Roswita was enthusiastic. "Yeah, Walter, let's go swimming."

"I don't go in the water," said Beatrix. "You go ahead. I'll just sit here."

"Right," said Vicky. "I haven't even unpacked my bathing suit."

211

"I might take a dip," said Gustav. "How about you, Ben?"

"Sure, why not?"

"Anywhere that whore goes, he follows," Beatrix started up again.

"Another word from you, I swear, I'll…"

"Throw me overboard? Is that what you were going to say?"

"I swear, I—I do something. Believe me."

Karl defused the heated exchange. "This place is full of colorful tropical fish. Like a damn aquarium down there."

Katja from the Ukraine and Roswita were ready; they had never worn anything but their bikinis on board.

Arriving at secluded Christmas Cove, Pat O'Neil was the first overboard, with mask and fins. Katja and Roswita followed. Britt rigged a ladder to get the swimmers back on board, and Karl launched the dinghy to be ready in case of an emergency. Walter, who did not snorkel, dove in for a swim. Ben and Gustav used the ladder to gradually lower themselves into the pleasantly cool water. Ben had given up trying to control his wife's drinking. While the swimmers frolicked in the water, she filled her glass with the rum punch Britt had left unattended. The incurable alcoholic that she was, small amounts of liquor sufficed to rob her of sound judgment. In her inebriated state she told Vicky, "Before he throws me overboard, I throw him overboard. And her, too. They can both go to hell."

Karl blew his whistle. "All out of the water! All out of the water!" Black clouds gathered and daylight faded, although it was just five o'clock. "We'll have a thunderstorm."

Gustav clambered up the ladder. "Hand me that towel please, Vicky. Oooh, it's cold, it's cold. The water is warmer than the air."

Walter and Roswita climbed into the dinghy that was tied to the stern of the *SEA WITCH*, while the others went back on board.

"Roswita, I am in an awkward position. Pat sees me as his rival. More than that, as an enemy. He is infatuated with you. He bumped into me, accidentally, you know, hit me with his fins, to provoke me. And Ben Gould scowls at me. He practically declared war back there on Virgin Gorda. Those two. There is something brewing between them. Ben thinks he can have you any time he wants. The older man versus his young rival. And I am in the middle."

"Only a couple more days, and all this is behind us. I will ignore Pat, but I can't ignore Ben, Walter, or I am out of business."

"Is your career that important to you? But why, Roswita? Not for the money?"

"Walter, I am thirty-eight. How much longer do I have?"

Karl called down to them. "Better come out of the dinghy now."

"Coming!" Walter yelled back. "And, Roswita, that lunatic Beatrix..." The first lightning struck, followed by crashing thunder. Walter and Roswita joined the others in the cockpit. Heavy downpour pelted the bimini top.

"We will wait until the weather clears, then sail into Cruz Bay," Karl announced.

"Or we could stay here overnight," Gustav proposed. "If it is safe, of course. Karl, what do you say?"

"Good idea. Who needs Cruz Bay?" said Pat. "We go back in the water when the storm is over. Is there something to eat? Perhaps Britt can whip something up. And how about a pitcher of margaritas, huh?"

Lightning was now all around them; the thunder rolled on and the rain came down in gusts. The *SEA WITCH* bucked on her anchor. Walter would have preferred to head for Cruz Bay, but he was outnumbered; both Katja and Roswita wanted to stay at Christmas Cove, and Karl said, "No problem."

Britt served roast beef and potato salad, and bottled Heinekens. "I'll make some margaritas for afterwards," she said to Pat.

"Yes, plenty of margaritas."

The storm lasted until after six. When the rain stopped, it was dark and the pitcher of margaritas empty. Katja from the Ukraine shamelessly fondled Walter, Roswita sat on Ben's lap, Pat O'Neil was isolated. He gulped the rest of his drink and stood up, a little unsteadily. "Back in the water!" It sounded like an order. "Where's my snorkel? My fins? Oh, what the hell, I don't need them."

"I advise against it," Karl cautioned. "It's dark, you had a lot to drink…"

Katja from the Ukraine said, "I like to be a little tipsy."

"Me too," giggled Roswita.

"If you go, I'll go," said Ben.

Walter thought, this looks like trouble. "Roswita, careful. I'll be in the dinghy. Stay close. Or better, don't go at all."

Drunk and careless, they jumped in. Ben followed, using the steps. Karl turned on the spreader lights, illuminating the deck and the water a few feet around the boat.

Walter went down into the dinghy. He observed Pat diving, coming up for air and diving again. He saw Roswita and Katja splashing. Then they were out of the circle of light, but he could still hear them. Ben Gould was in the water, holding on to the ladder.

Karl, on the stern of the *SEA WITCH*, turned on a spotlight and found Pat pulling Katja back toward the boat.

Chapter Nineteen

"US Coast Guard, US Coast Guard, US Coast Guard. This is the SEA WITCH. Over." Karl used the emergency channel. He repeated the call.

"This is the US Coast Guard station at Borinquen, Puerto Rico. SEA WITCH, what is your emergency? Over."

"US documented sailing vessel SEA WITCH. Anchored at Christmas Cove, USVI. One person overboard. Repeat: one person overboard. Not located. Over."

"Stand by." There was silence on board the *SEA WITCH*. Everybody suddenly was sober. Then the voice came back on the VHF radio. "SEA WITCH, we are dispatching helicopter HU25 to the scene. ETA 1905. Over."

"Acknowledged. Standing by on channel six. Out."

Karl, equipped with his spotlight, had crisscrossed the area in the Zodiac before making the call to the US Coast Guard. Now he went back once more on the search, taking Walter with him. "There are strong, unpredictable currents running between these little islets. They depend on a combination of tide and wind conditions. We'll find her. Is she a good swimmer?"

"No. I mean, she can stay afloat, treading water or floating on her back, but swimming? Not really."

"She might have become disoriented. She drank a lot. Never a good idea."

They heard the helicopter and, unsuccessful in their search, returned to the boat.

Chopper HU25 hovered over the scene, turning night into day with a powerful spotlight. Then the beat of the rotor blades slowly faded into the distance. Karl said, "They follow the current."

Helplessness and hope, gloom and optimism, uncertainty and suspicion pervaded the atmosphere in the cockpit of the *SEA WITCH*. And silence.

The VHF radio crackled and startled the group. "SEA WITCH, SEA WITCH. This is the US Coast Guard. Over."

Karl spoke into the mike. "SEA WITCH listening. Over."

"HU25 was unsuccessful in her search and returns to base. A local official from nearby Red Hook, St. Thomas is underway to Christmas Cove. You are to follow the instructions of the local authorities. Over."

"Understood. Thanks for your assistance. SEA WITCH out."

"That's it?" Walter was incredulous. "That's it? Does that mean..."

"The search is over. It's been nearly two hours."

"But she might have been washed ashore somewhere," said Katja. "I was with her, and then I lost her in the dark. I called, but... I didn't hear her." She sobbed. "Then Pat pulled me away."

A motorboat appeared from behind one of the rocky islets and closed in on the *SEA WITCH*. On board were a policeman and a civilian. "Evening," said the civilian. "Coast Guard called and sent me out here. You having some trouble?"

"Yes. I am Karl Miller, the skipper. We lost one of our charter group. They were swimming just a few feet from the boat, then one female disappeared. We searched, the helicopter searched—nothing. It's been two hours now."

"May I come on board? I am the marshal over at Red Hook. I have to make a report."

"Come on board."

"A report? You are not doing anything about it? What kind of a report?" Walter was outraged. "We have to find her. She's out there, alone, and you want to make a report?"

"Sir, with all due respect, it is night, she's gone for two hours, you searched, the Coast Guard searched. What is there for me to do? I have to report the incident to Charlotte Amalie. Now, let me talk to the skipper." He turned back to Karl. "Can you give me some details? When it happened, how it happened, who was there, who saw her last. Things like that."

"What is your name?" Walter insisted; everyone else was in awe or in shock. "I'll report you. You come out here and do nothing? Who is your superior?"

Karl said as calmly as he could, "Mr. Hansen, let me handle it. Please." He turned back to the marshal. "Come below, please. I'll give you the details as I know them."

After a while, Karl called for Katja. "Please, tell the marshal what happened."

"We were swimming, Mr. Marshal, and then I didn't see her anymore. That's all I know. You think she might have drowned? But why, why? Then there was Pat."

"There is a strong current running, especially after a storm," he said. "Who did you say was there?"

"Pat. I mean, Mr. O'Neil. He is a good swimmer. He pulled me back to the boat."

219

"I want to talk to him," said the marshal. "You may go. Tell Mr. O'Neil to come down here."

Pat showed a defiant attitude. "What do you want to know? I saved one person, didn't I? I didn't see Roswita, eh, Miss Peschel. The current was fierce. I did what I could." He went back up the companionway. "Is he accusing me?" Pat looked at those assembled in the cockpit. "Me? I did what I could."

Gustav Melchior spoke. "Nobody is accusing you. Perhaps, Pat, perhaps you could have tried... I mean, you are a strong swimmer."

"Now you are accusing me, too. There was no more I could have done. I did not see or hear her." He looked at Walter. "And you, you did nothing. Just sat in the dinghy. Why didn't you do something?

"I had no idea that there was a problem. Only you knew."

"You... I don't believe you. Your attitude has irritated me long enough."

Beatrix came out of her stupor. "Ben, why are you so quiet? Because your whore is dead? I could have told you it's coming to a bad end."

"Shut up. She's not dead." He pleaded for support. "She's not dead, right? Katja? Vicky? She's not dead, right?"

Silence.

"Well, skipper, I am done here. Keep the radio open. The prefecture in Charlotte Amalie will contact you within the hour." The marshal climbed up the companionway into the cockpit. "Evening," he said. No one answered. His boat whisked him away into the night.

Then all spoke at once. What will happen now? She may still be alive. Will there be an investigation? Can they arrest us? Who is under suspicion? We all are. But she may still be alive. Was it an accident, or was there foul play? Who is to blame? Who? Who wanted her dead? We don't know; she may be alive.

One thought repeated itself over and over in Walter's mind: But why, Roswita?

"Listen up," Karl demanded attention. "I declare a state of emergency on board this vessel. There will be no liquor. No disruptive behavior. No blaming or accusing. We wait for further instructions from the authorities." Then he called his company, Island Charters, to report the incident.

By midnight, the prefecture ordered him to return the SEA WITCH directly to Charlotte Amalie. The crew and all passengers were once more interrogated and then released.

Island Charters, the company that owned the SEA WITCH, fired both Karl, the skipper, and the mate Britt, for reasons of irresponsibility and not adhering to the sail plan. He had deviated from the predetermined itinerary to sail from Jost Van Dyke to Cruz Bay, St. John. The more serious accusation, however, was to allow the passengers in his charge to swim at night in an area of known dangerous currents, especially after consuming copious amounts of alcohol.

The District Court ruled the tragic incident an accident and no criminal charges were brought against Karl Miller or Island Charters.

In an interview with the reporter from a local paper, Karl stated that he had intended to sail directly to Cruz Bay, but agreed to a stop for an hour at Christmas Cove. "We had time to reach Cruz Bay in daylight, but were pinned down by a thunderstorm." Then he related the often bizarre behavior of his passengers. "There was a lot of drinking, hostility and switching sex partners. They were the weirdest bunch of people I ever had to deal with." Asked, if he had any suspicion that it might not have been an accident, he hesitated. The reporter pressed him on that question. "Do you think it is possible? You mentioned sex and hostility," to which Karl answered, "Could be, but I can't say."

Rumors, although quite plausible, had it that the St. Thomas reporter sold the list of passengers on that fateful cruise to a New York based tabloid. Walter Hansen's telephone rang early in the morning after his return to New York. The caller requested an interview regarding the drowning of Roswita Peschel. Walter declined.

That day, under the headline *The bizarre Disappearance of Roswita Peschel*, an article in the tabloid posed the question, *Accident or Murder?* and contained almost verbatim what Karl had told the reporter in St. Thomas. The last line of the article was a devastating blow for Walter. *Walter Hansen, VP of Automotive Imports & Distribution, and steady companion of the late Roswita Peschel, declined an interview.*

Love. That word was never spoken between Roswita and Walter. Their relationship had been the most honest, unpretentious bond two people can have. There were no lies, no false promises, no obligations. Instead, there was understanding.

Walter realized that what they had was love in the purest form. His name in the paper next to that of Roswita was now the only remnant of that love. The quote *steady companion of the late Roswita Peschel* did not remain unnoticed. Snippets of their life style came to light and were overstated with relish. Subsequent articles in various tabloids intimated his possible involvement in her presumed drowning, and fueled the desire of readers to see someone fall, especially someone in a high position.

The fall came a week later. AID relieved Walter Hansen from his position as vice president. The legal department drafted an agreement to secure avoidance of possible legal action, which Walter signed in exchange for a substantial severance amount.

Even in Germany, the story of Walter Hansen and Roswita Peschel was picked up by some of the more sensationalist papers. It was unlikely that Walter's mother had knowledge of her son's double life, other than by mother's intuition. She died before the circumstances of Roswita's demise filtered into German tabloids.

Walter did not attend his mother's funeral. He had not been present at his father's funeral, which was accepted grudgingly by the family, but his absence when his mother was laid to rest, met with disapproval. His uncle wrote, demanding an explanation for the callous disrespect of family values. He had read of his nephew's extravagant life style and the question surrounding the disappearance of his mistress, and added, "This is not the way of our family." Walter was not inclined to justify his actions or neglects. He still asked himself the question: But why, Roswita? He could find no answer.

Gerda Chang, long ignored by him, called. "Is it true?"

"Yes. She was my friend, and she drowned. Her body was not found. I have nothing to add."

Katja from the Ukraine left Schuster & O'Neil. She contacted Walter and told him that Schuster terminated his partnership with Pat.

Walter never called on Gustav Melchior or Ben Gould, and Pat O'Neil had good reason to keep his distance from all his cruise companions; he was not free from their suspicion.

Once more Katja called Walter. "Pat moved to California." Walter was not interested. "You want to get together some time?" He was not interested in that either.

Helen Rossi asked, "What happened? I can't believe it."

"Neither can I."

Walter contemplated what to do with the rest of his life. The tabloids had planted false suspicion and tarnished his reputation in the business world.

Money was no object for him. He did not need a job. He spent the days sailing in his *ROXY II*, alone. At other times, he drove long distances out of town, avoiding places that reminded him of Roswita.

His luxury apartment on Seventy-ninth Street felt too big and he longed for the studio on Thirty-fifth Street, or his room at Mrs. Nieves's boarding place. Back to the beginning, he thought, and wondered how Nilda was doing. Even further back he went in his ruminations. Vienna held no special memories, and so his thoughts returned to the carefree time in Frankfurt. Ilse. He could not remember her last name; she was just Ilse. I had friends then, he smiled sadly.

His phone rang. He let the machine take it. "Hi. It's Felicia. Felicia Napolitano. Remember me?" He went to pick it up.

"Yes, I remember you. How are you?"

"Walter, I just found out about it. What happened? Are you all right? It's over a month."

"Yes. Over a month. I still can't talk about it. Nice of you to call."

"Wait, Walter. I can't believe Roxy is gone. I am so sorry."

"Felicia, perhaps some other time."

Weeks later, on a Saturday morning, they met in a café on Second Avenue. He told her the whole story. The drinking, the sex, the rivalry, the suspicions. "Yes, I have suspicions, but it was ruled an accident, and that is what I have to believe."

"I want to believe that, too. It would drive me insane to think that she was murdered. But, from what you are telling me…" Felicia looked at her watch. "I'd better get going. I have a flight to Frankfurt tonight. A few things to take care of."

"Yes, sure."

They hugged and said good-bye.

He stood at the curb and saw Felicia getting into a taxi. His mind drifted. Frankfurt, she said. She has a flight to Frankfurt.

* * *

Walter Hansen was forty-three when he resolved to return to Frankfurt, the city he had left some twenty years before. Get away from this whirlpool of suspicions and doubts, implications and finger pointing. The party is over.

In the winter of 1972/73, he registered *ROXY II* with a yacht brokerage. In April, she was sold for forty-eight thousand dollars, the same price he had paid four years earlier. The real estate market was in a slump that year and Walter lost a considerable amount in the sale of the Seventy-ninth Street apartment he and Roswita had shared.

His arrangements finished, he bid farewell to New York, the city that saw him struggling at first, and then climbing to prominence and financial independence. And how did he see New York? As a sorceress, a beautiful and dangerous temptress. As a city that promises and deceives, gives and takes away.

He had left Germany as a young man, full of expectations. Now he returned to his homeland, expecting nothing.

LaVergne, TN USA
26 August 2010
194851LV00003B/26/P